RED FLAGS AND BUTTERFLIES

RED FLAGS AND BUTTERFLIES

SHERYL AZZAM

DCB

Second printing, February 2026.

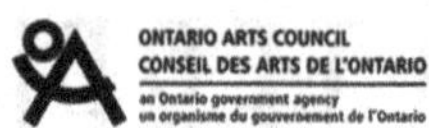

We acknowledge financial support for our publishing activities: the Government of Canada, through the Canada Book Fund and The Canada Council for the Arts; the Government of Ontario, through the Ontario Arts Council, Ontario Creates, and the Ontario Book Publishing Tax Credit.

Library and Archives Canada Cataloguing in Publication

Title: Red flags and butterflies / Sheryl Azzam.
Names: Azzam, Sheryl, author.
Identifiers: Canadiana (print) 20250172135 | Canadiana (ebook) 20250172208 | ISBN 9781770868069 (softcover) | ISBN 9781770868076 (EPUB)
Subjects: LCGFT: Novels.
Classification: LCC PS8601.Z93 R43 2025 | DDC jC813/.6—dc23

United States Library of Congress Control Number: 2025934331

Cover and interior text design: Marijke Friesen
Manufactured by Copywell in Woodbridge,
Ontario in February 2026.

Printed using paper from a responsible and sustainable resource, including a mix of virgin fibres and recycled materials.

Printed and bound in Canada.

EU RP eucomply OÜ
Pärnu mnt 139b-14, 11317 Tallinn, Estonia
hello@eucompliancepartner.com, +3375690241

DCB Young Readers
An imprint of Cormorant Books Inc.
260 Ishpadinaa (Spadina) Avenue, Suite 502, Tkaronto (Toronto), ON M5T 2E4, Canada

Suite 110, 7068 Portal Way, Ferndale, WA 98248, USA

www.dcbyoungreaders.com
info@cormorantbooks.com / www.cormorantbooks.com

CHAPTER ONE

SATURDAY, OCTOBER 14

With his legs split apart, he grabs his ankles and drops his head between his knees. Water droplets slide off his back, forming a puddle underneath him. I let my eyes travel up his sleek, clearly defined legs as he stands and reaches for the ceiling with his right arm. Folding it over his head, he grabs his elbow with his left hand and pulls it down for a deep stretch of his triceps. He does the same with the other arm before he falls into a side abdominal stretch, and I can't help but appreciate his well-toned obliques, and how his chestnut-colored hair falls over his eyes as he bends sideways.

I know I'm staring but I can't help it. My eyes won't listen.

He straightens and smooths his hair back into place over his head, and his eyes lock on mine. My face flushes and I look away. I count three Mississippis before I risk another peek, only to find that he's still looking at me, and electric sparks race up and down my arms, like a bunch of tiny firecrackers exploding. He gives me a sly smile and what I think is a slight nod at the same time that Zara's elbow crushes into my ribs.

"Stop staring at him and pay attention. Coach will be peeved if you don't know the drill when we get in the pool. Keep your eye on the prize, okay?"

"Oh, don't worry. My eye's most definitely on the prize."

"Not THAT prize."

"Lexie, you got something to say?" Coach fixes his gaze on me, taps his clipboard against his thigh.

I freeze. The whole team is looking at me. *He's* looking at me.

"Uh, no, Coach."

"Good," he says. "Because you need to practice this more than anyone. I want you to swim it at Spring Regionals. You got that?"

Zara squeezes my elbow and lets out a tiny squeal that only I can hear.

"Got it. Thanks, Coach."

"Good." He blows his whistle. "Everybody in the pool."

"You know what that means, don't you?" Zara pushes through the door to the change room and answers her own question for me. "There's most definitely a scholarship with your name on it."

"Maybe," I say. "But that's assuming I get accepted."

She rolls her eyes. "Like that'll be a problem, Little Miss Ninety Average."

She turns on the shower and stands under it. I turn on the one next to her, crank it to almost scalding, and squeeze some shampoo from the dispenser into my hand.

"The caveat, though, is that you actually have to submit your application. Tell me you've told your dad you're applying."

My stomach twists when she says that, and her wide, almond-shaped, coffee-brown eyes, framed by her perfectly plucked eyebrows, bore into mine.

"I need for us to both be at Sunridge next year, Lexie. I've waited long enough for us to be in the same school," she says, as if the fact that we've been going to different schools for the past four years has caused her some injury.

"Yes. I know. I'm working on it."

I stick my head under the water, my attempt to make this line of conversation go away. Her and Mom's constant reminders to "just tell him already" are getting on my last nerve. I don't need a reminder about something that occupies my thoughts 24-7. What I need is a way to get Dad onboard with the idea of me switching schools so I could attend Sunridge High's School of Fine Art and Music. It's not like I haven't been trying to tell him. I first mentioned it to him a year ago when Mr. Harris suggested it. "What would he know about it?" Dad had asked at the time. "He's just an old man in a nursing home."

I tried to explain to him that Mr. Harris was a lot more than that. His late husband had been an instructor at Sunridge. Mr. Harris knew the program, and he'd seen my work. He said that I was the perfect candidate for Sunridge High's Fine Art and Music program. My art teacher agreed when I asked her. She said that it would be a great stepping stone toward getting a masters in curatorial studies, and that with my swimming, I could likely get at least some of the tuition covered with a sports scholarship. It was, quite literally, like the program was made for me. Mom agrees. Dad, though? Not so much. He doesn't like the idea of a high school education that you have to pay for, and he especially doesn't like that it's in my mom's part of town, so I'd need to live with her. He thinks he's being generous enough by letting me be part of a swim club in that area.

Zara turns off the water and bends to the side, squeezing water from the length of her wavy, cinnamon-streaked, dark brown hair. Then she asks her question again, the one she's been asking over and over, each time with the words rearranged in a different order like she thinks that'll somehow make me give her the answer that'll explain everything.

"I still don't understand what the issue is. It's one of the most prestigious programs around. Why wouldn't he want you to go?"

I lift my shoulder, try to pretend it's not a big deal even though it is, because the truth is, I don't even know. The few times that I tried to discuss it with him, the subject somehow got changed, or he'd remind me of all the benefits of my current school, which, fair enough, are good, but they're not art school good. Comparing them is like comparing good art pencils with dollar store pencils. Totally different, like not even on the same planet. I've tried to explain to her that Dad doesn't always see things the way other people do, and that he needs time to come around to the idea. She always nods like she gets it, but I know she doesn't. It's my fault though. I can never explain it properly. Every time I think I've finally found the right words, I can't figure out how to arrange them so they make the most sense.

"I'm going to swing by the marina and check on Nate," I say, changing the subject. "Want to come?"

Her face clouds over. "I can't. Mom's physiotherapist is coming. But are you sure Nate's ready to see friends? Are you sure you're ready for that?"

I pin a smile on my face, try to force the swell of emotion that rises in my throat away. It's been eleven days since my last shift at the marina with Nate and his grandfather, "Pops," and ten since Nate found Pops slumped over in his La-Z-Boy, his pencil still in his hand, his crossword puzzles spilled on the floor around him. It's been hard for me to accept that I'll never again get to work alongside him, crafting another canoe, or tackling his mounds of paperwork. How was it possible that I'd never hear him ask me for a seven-letter word for something ever again, or what genus a particular species of bird falls under?

"The funeral was a week ago, so I hope so. There's something I need to give him. Besides, I'm sure the office needs my attention. All that paperwork isn't going to take care of itself."

The lights are on when I enter the office at the marina, so I know Nate's around.

"Nate?" My voice echoes through the office and into the deserted shop behind it. As I suspected, everything is exactly as I left it, like the place is frozen in time.

The bucket that I put on the floor in the middle of the shop to catch the rainwater is still there, the water in it a couple of inches deep, and my old fishing boat is still in front of the double-wide garage door where Pops and I left it after he helped me prep it for painting. The lump in my throat gets thick again when I think about him, and I try to swallow it away.

I found the boat last spring when I took one of Pops's canoes out on the lake. The ice had barely relinquished its grip on the water when I saw it moored on its side, hidden in the reeds, covered in a layer of green slime. I instantly knew the treasure I'd found. It was just like the boat that Dad used to have, that he took Jonah and me out fishing every weekend in, before it was awarded to Mom in the divorce. My plan was to gift it to Dad for his birthday. I knew it would be, hands down, better than anything Jonah would give him. I got Nate to help me haul it out of the sucking mud and carry it to the shop, and Pops was happy to help me with it, a project right up his alley.

On the desk in the office, the paperwork I organized into folders is still stacked beside the computer, the book for signing out canoes still open to the last entry I recorded eleven days ago.

"You don't need to make that so complicated, you know. I've told you that before," Pops said, after watching me log the details of one of the canoes I rented out that day.

"Yes, I do, Pops," I said. "And logging the details isn't complicated. Do I need to remind you about what happened to some of your canoes before you hired me to start keeping track of them?"

He snorted, like it was me being ridiculous, and shuffled back into the shop.

I knew he was just teasing. That he appreciated the way I'd turned his office into a well-oiled machine. That he needed and relied on me, like I did on him and the marina.

Back when Mom, Jonah, and I first moved here when I was eleven, Pops would find me almost every day after school, fishing off the end of his dock. It became my favorite place to chill out from the stress of Mom and Dad's divorce. I didn't know I was trespassing. He made a deal with me that I could use his dock and canoes whenever I wanted if I helped him in the office on the weekends. It's how I became his right hand in terms of managing all things marina.

I find Nate sitting at the end of the dock, his legs dangling over the water.

"Hey," I say, sliding in beside him. I nudge his foot with mine. "You okay?"

He keeps his eyes trained on the water while he nods and sighs a sigh that I know means he's not okay. "Yeah. Are you?"

Tears clog my throat. "I'm okay like you are, I guess."

He grabs my hand and squeezes it, and we sit in silence for a minute or ten, remembering.

"I brought this for you," I say, pulling the frame I'd wrapped in tissue from my bag and handing it to him. "I think you and your dad should have it."

His eyes go soft and, I'm pretty sure, a bit damp, but he looks away from me. He knows what it is. It's the first watercolor that I've ever attempted, that I've spent the last few weekends working on, before and after my shifts at the marina. Usually I sketch in one of my Moleskine sketchbooks using either my Staedtler Mars pencils or charcoal, but for this one, I bought an 11 × 14 canvas and decided to try a watercolor mimicking the style of Michal Jasiewicz and paint Pops in one of his canoes, fishing along the reeds of the marsh. It took me longer than I expected to finish it, but the extra time was worth it, and I'm glad Ms. Wilcox urged me to try it.

"I can't take this. You said it was for your portfolio, for your application to the art school."

I shake my head. "It belongs here. I'll paint something else for my portfolio."

He squeezes my hand, a silent thanks, and a breeze blows through, bringing with it the scent of sweet clover and moss.

"He bought the OldMill," he says.

My mind races. I'd heard Pops mention that he wanted to buy it. It was part of his plan to attract more people to this end of the lake again. Ever since the city built a new marina on the north side of the lake, people stopped coming down here, and business dried up. I never took it seriously, though. After working alongside him in the office, I knew it wasn't something he could afford. I think of the stack of paper, the bills in the "to be paid" folder. I organized them in order of importance, if there even was such a thing, because which one wasn't important? The ones stamped with third and final notice I labeled with bright yellow Post-it flags and filed them on top, leaving the most recent and by virtue of that, I rationalized, less important at the back. I also think about the collection agency that keeps calling about some long overdue payment, and Pops telling me not to worry about it. That he had it under control.

"Where did he get the money?"

Nate shrugs. "Doesn't matter. What matters is that it's our problem now, and we can't even afford this place, never mind that one too." He huffs in frustration. "I don't know how we're going to do it. My dad's super stressed. He's taken a second job, and he's in talks with the bank about getting a loan to help cover the costs of this place and the cost of renovating the OldMill, but we might not get approved. We might have to sell everything."

My breath snags. "You can't sell. This place was everything to him."

Worry lines his face. "It is to me too."

I want to tell him not to worry, but my throat coats with tears again. I know I don't need to tell him that the marina is everything to me too.

CHAPTER TWO

WEDNESDAY, OCTOBER 18

"Your regular, Lexie?" Glen, the Chip Wagon guy, asks me.

"Yes, please."

"And Zara, too?"

"Nope. Just me today."

We've stopped at the wagon practically every week since we started swimming together, but today Zara had to rush home to help her mom. I always get the fries with extra ketchup and an iced tea; Zara gets the double-loaded poutine with a diet Coke.

Glen's arm stretches over the counter to pass me my order, which is when I realize that my money's in the pocket of my other hoodie, which is currently in a heap on my bedroom floor. Crap.

"I'm sorry, Glen. I forgot my money. Can I make up for it on Sat —"

"I got it. Don't worry," says a voice from behind me. An arm stretches over me to pass Glen a five-dollar bill. Turning, I find Hot Lifeguard smiling at me. I swear, my life force pools in my feet and my throat starts to manufacture dust. He's changed out of his red lifeguard shirt into an azul blue T-shirt that makes his eyes look like I want to swim in them. The rescue float that was slung over his shoulder has been replaced with a guitar case. I manage to croak out a thanks and take my order from Glen.

"No problem." His slow smile makes time freeze, but my heart beats a bazillion times a minute. I now have serious doubts that I'll even be able to eat the fries he just paid for.

"I saw you swim just now. You've got good form."

Oh jeez.

His eyes are fixed on mine, and I know it's my turn to say something, but it's not every day that the Hot Lifeguard who pops up out of nowhere to pay for your fries compliments you, so the only thing I can think of to say is the same thing I already said.

"Uh, thanks."

Stupid. Stupid. Stupid. Is that the only thing you know how to say?

"I heard your coach tell you last week that he wants you to swim the fly at Spring Regionals."

What's going on? Why is he talking to me?

"Um, yeah."

He nods. "That's cool. I swim the fly too. Or, I mean, I used to. Before I tore my rotator cuff."

"Yikes. That must've hurt."

Ugh. You're such a loser.

He laughs. "It did. But I don't swim anymore. Well, I do, obviously, but not competitively. I'm Rhys, by the way."

I smile at him.

"And you are . . . ?"

"Oh, Lexie! I'm Lexie."

Idiot. Idiot. Idiot.

"Thanks for the fries. I'll pay you back."

"Don't worry about it." His eyes break from mine, seem to sweep over me, but it happens so fast, I probably imagined it. "How come I've never seen you around before? Are you new here?"

"No. I go to Greenbay, on my dad's side of town. But I'm applying to Sunridge's Art and Music program — it's just a couple of blocks away from here — so hopefully I'll be around more next year."

He nods. "I know some people applying to that. It sounds competitive."

"It is. You're not applying?" My eyes land on his guitar case. "It looks like music's your thing."

He shrugs. "Music, yes. A fancy music program that's not going to help my band get a record deal, no." His left eye quivers. I think it might be a wink. "But if you're applying, maybe I'll have to reconsider."

My face gets hot and a couple of seconds tick by like years before I realize it's my turn to speak. Thankfully he speaks first.

"Maybe we could swim together sometime?"

The dust in my throat chokes off my words.

Um, what?

"I just thought that I might be able to help you improve your form even more. Given that I used to lay down a pretty good fly, I might be of help."

My eyes want to pop wide open over the fact that Hot Lifeguard is, I'm pretty sure, asking me out, but I don't let them. I force them to stay their normal size so he doesn't change his mind because I look like a starstruck idiot.

"Yeah. Sure. Okay," I hear myself say.

He beams a satisfied smile and bounces back on his heels. "Great. How about next week? Maybe after your practice?"

"Sure," I say, trying hard to force the squeak from my voice. An awkward moment passes while I stare at him.

"I'll see you next week then," he says, taking a step back. "I'm late for band practice."

My head bobs up and down, and I watch him walk away wondering what a hot guy like him wants with a regular girl like me.

CHAPTER THREE

SATURDAY, OCTOBER 21

It's been three days since Rhys sort-of-but-didn't ask me out at the chip wagon, and I feel like my feet haven't properly touched the ground since. I saw him at practice this morning, but he was busy with his supervisor, and by the time Coach let us go, he was gone. I wasn't sure whether to be relieved or disappointed. I've been thinking about him constantly, wondering about all sorts of things like who his favorite bands are, whether he prefers Coke or Pepsi, skinny or fat Cheezies (definitely skinny), if he has any pets, what he likes to watch on Netflix, and whether he prefers toast or cereal for breakfast. What I have found out is that he's in grade ten just like me, and that he's the lead guitarist in a band called the Raging Rhinos.

I force thoughts of him out of my mind, though, because it's Dad's weekend again, and I need to get straight in my head how I'm going to tell him about my plan to apply to Sunridge. Enough putting it off. I think about what Zara said when we FaceTimed last night, and of course she's right. I'm letting thoughts of how I *think* he'll react stress me out. Once I explain it all properly, show him the materials, there's no way he'll be able to say no. I'm making mountains out of molehills again, like Dad says I do. It's why Mom insists I go to therapy.

Shoving away the queasy feeling that's creeping into my gut, I slip my weekend essentials into my backpack along with my Moleskine sketchbook, my drawing pencils, and my chemistry textbook. I need to finish a couple of sketches for my portfolio and study for my chem test on Monday. The sketches will be easy; the chem stuff, not so much. I still don't know why I decided to take AP Chemistry as one of my electives. I'm pretty sure it hates me as much as I hate it.

Zipping my backpack closed, I dump the last of the water from my watering can onto the soil of my potted fern, grab my hoodie from the end of my bed, and head downstairs.

"How was practice?" Mom asks.

"It was brutal. That fly is going to kill me. I need to get to the pool more often." I lower my voice so Jonah can't hear me. "Especially if I want that scholarship."

Mom nods and her eyes flicker to Jonah. He's focused on the street outside, waiting for Dad's car to come around the corner. He doesn't know about my plans, and I don't want him to, because he'll make it his business to tell Dad before I get the chance.

"Jonah," Mom says, wiping a plate dry with a towel. "You're going to ask your dad to help you with your science project this weekend, right?"

He gives a who-cares shrug. "It's a waste of time. Especially since I'm going to be a motocross driver. Dad said I could."

I suppress the urge to roll my eyes. Getting Jonah to do his homework is like trying to convince a cat to eat vegetables.

Mom's lips press together. "That's fine. But you still need to get your homework done."

He talks over her, like he doesn't hear her. "He also said that my dirt bike is ready. He went to the Auto Parts Depot and got a new carburetor for it. It runs much better now and doesn't stall out. He says he'll take me out to ride it."

I shift my gaze to Mom, see her stiffen as she stacks the now-dry plates back in the cupboard. Her face has that pinched look that means she's got more to say but won't say it. She's hated that dirt bike since the day Dad bought it last winter. It's never worked, and even if Jonah knew how to ride it, he can't because it's way too big for him. I'm not a fan of it either, since Dad bought it after he told me he couldn't afford to pay his share of my swim club dues.

"All right," she says, dragging a smile to her lips, "just don't forget to wear the helmet I —"

"He's here," Jonah says, flinging the door open.

"Wait! Take a bag of groceries with you, please." Mom hands him one of two bags she had set aside next to the door.

He grumbles, but takes it before he flies out the door, shoes in his other hand. "See ya!"

I stuff my feet in my Crocs and take the bag of groceries Mom offers me.

"I'll try to remind him about his homework," I say.

"Thanks, but that's not your job."

"I know, but maybe if I remind him, he'll at least do a little bit of it."

"Don't worry about his responsibilities. You've got enough of your own to worry about."

My stomach flips. She doesn't have to say it for me to know what her eyes are telling me. I can't help asking, though. Like somehow if she tells me what I want to hear, it'll erase the likelihood that he'll say no. Even though I know it's ridiculous, a small part of me is superstitious enough to think it might work.

"Do you think he'll be okay with it?"

The words hiding behind her eyes tell me that she's thought a lot about it. She opens her mouth to say something, but Dad lays on the horn and makes hand gestures telling me to hurry up. Jonah follows his lead. A hardness flutters across Mom's eyes, but then just as quickly it's gone, and whatever she was going to say, she now isn't.

"Of course. Don't worry. Have fun with your dad at the fair."

I slide the groceries and my backpack into the back seat and climb in beside them. I've barely closed the door before Dad's reversing down the driveway. He and Jonah are so engrossed in their conversation, he doesn't even look back to say hello.

"Mmmm. This is, like, the best corn dog ever," Jonah says, wiping ketchup from his chin.

"You always say that."

"That's because it's always true." He smirks at me.

We're sitting under the massive food tent at one of the dozens of picnic tables with our traditional fair food: Jonah, a corn dog, chili fries, and iced root beer; me, a gluten-free funnel cake with cinnamon sugar, whipped cream, and strawberry sauce with a lemon slushie; and Dad, sampling a few of the prize-winning chilis from the chili cook-off with a pint of Molson Canadian.

I don't know how he can eat that in this heat. Just looking at the steam rising from it is enough to make me start sweating again. It seems that even though it's late October, the weather fairies haven't gotten the memo, because it's still as hot as midsummer at five p.m. I slip my feet out of my Crocs and bury them in the cool grass under the table. After walking on the dusty, compacted gravel floor of the midway for the last three hours, they feel like they're two sizes bigger than they actually are.

We've been coming to the fall fair ever since I can remember, and I don't think it's ever been this hot and dry. Mom used to come with us, and if she were here, she'd be eating a funnel cake like me. We come with just Dad now. Mom says that since it's always been Dad's thing to take us, he should be the one to continue doing it.

He sips his beer and makes a show of putting it down on the opposite side of the table, away from Jonah.

"What?" Jonah mumbles around a mouthful of corn dog.

"Nothing. I'm just putting my beer over here, far away from you."

Jonah freezes, a look of incredulity on his face. "I didn't knock it over! You did!"

"Whatever. It was an accident. You don't need to lie about it."

"I'm not lying!" Jonah's corn dog slaps onto his plate.

Dad's eyes narrow, like they do when he thinks someone is overreacting. His eyes dart about the tent.

"Watch yourself. You're getting all bent out of shape for nothing. I'm just teasing —"

Dad's got a weird sense of humor and Jonah hasn't learned to not take the bait.

"So, what do you want to do now?" I interrupt, before things get out of control.

The shift in both of them is immediate. The broodiness lifts from Dad's eyes and Jonah forgets that he's angry, as I knew he would.

Dad swallows another spoonful of chili. "Let's get a spot on the grandstand for the demolition derby. If we go now, we'll get front row seats."

"I want to go back to the midway," says Jonah, popping the last of his corn dog into his mouth and licking his fingers. "I'm not leaving here until I win one of those green lizards. Did you see it? The one with the row of spikes down its back, that's as tall as me?"

Dad snorts and pulls a roll of cash secured with a rubber band from his pocket. I suck in my cheeks at the sight. "If that's what you want to do, I'd better get some more tickets. Lexie, which —"

The words are out before my brain reminds my mouth not to speak. "You've got money now? Because Mom got you groceries again."

His eyes land like frost on mine before his lips pull into a smile, thawing them. "Don't worry. I'll pay her back. I forgot to tell her I didn't need any this week."

I nod and look away. He'd better pay her back. I focus on the ice in the bottom of my cup, try to pretend I can't feel the weight of his stare.

"You didn't answer the question," he says, making my stomach fill with slush.

I force my eyes to his. "What question?"

"Which of those giant stuffed things do you want this year?"

The slush in my stomach melts away at his teasing tone. "I don't need one this year. I've still got the bear and the dog you won for me the last two years we came."

The truth is, I don't want him to spend more money that he doesn't have. I get it now. When we used to come with Mom, she would always try to limit us to a few games each, and it caused a fight between her and Dad every time. She'd always tell us that we were only going to buy a certain number of tickets, and once they were gone, that was it. We'd agree and tell her what she wanted to hear, but once those tickets were gone, all we had to do was smile and ask Dad with a "pretty please" to get more tickets, and it was a done deal. Mom's smile would disappear and she'd complain that he was wasting money on silly, impossible games, and he'd tell her she was being a control freak and that "our smiles were worth the money." He'd let us play as many games as we wanted, and then if we still didn't get the prize we were after, he'd play the game to win it for us. Every year Dad would walk out of the fairgrounds with at least one human-sized stuffed something or other on his shoulders, and every year all of us would hate Mom for being such a downer.

Dad rolls his eyes. "Nobody needs them, Lexie, but it's fun. Tradition. You pick one, and if you can't get it, I'll get it for you."

I know better than to argue, so I give him the response I know he expects and he pays a hundred bucks for sixty tickets and hands us each thirty. I look at the tickets in my hand and can't help seeing Mom's disapproving face. I need to choose a game I can actually win, so that Dad doesn't need to buy more tickets to get me the prize he's hell-bent on making sure I get.

I take my time and am wandering up and down the midway, searching for a game I might have a chance at winning easily, when I find Jonah under the Build-a-Boat tent, tongue sticking out in concentration as he works to secure tinfoil around the hull of the boat he crafted from a paper plate. I stand beside him, watching him work, and can't help but notice that the grand prize is, in fact, a giant green lizard.

"Five minutes left!" announces the game attendant from his place behind the counter.

"What do you think?" He hands me his paper boat. "It's better than all their boats, isn't it?" His eyes slide around to the other builders, pointing without pointing.

I turn it around in my hands, nod my head toward the kid on the other side of the table. "His boat has a sail. Where's yours?"

"Pffft," he says, making the hair on his forehead jump. "That boat's toast as soon as the sail gets wet."

I frown at him and shove my finger against my lips. He laughs.

"Wouldn't it be even cooler though," he says, "if I could sail this boat myself, like in those pictures?" He points to the side wall of the canvas tent.

I step away from him to get a closer look. There are about a dozen photos under a banner titled "Duct Tape Boat Regatta 2011–2018," and each shows a variety of life-size rafts made of cardboard and duct tape. There's a tugboat, a shark, an enormous flamingo, and one made to look like a pirate ship, and it occurs to me that running an event like this at the marina could be the perfect way to raise some much-needed extra money. I take photos of the photo wall and text them to Nate.

After sticking around to watch Jonah win his race, the three of us — that is, he, I, and the lizard — finally find a game that I think I can win. I smile at my luck. Its grand prize is a rainbow sunfish, and as far as giant stuffed animals go, it's one of the nicest. The game's called Rifle Range, and since I've gone with Dad to the shooting range a few times, I know my way around a rifle and target. With some concentration and luck, winning the fish should be easy. The idea is to shoot the gophers as they pop up out of their holes, but as I watch the guy ahead of me, my heart sinks. They pop up and disappear so fast, taking good aim is next to impossible.

I've just fired and missed my sixth shot when Dad appears behind us. "Which prize are you going for?"

Without taking my eyes off the gopher hole, I mumble out "fish" and pull the trigger.

Crap. Missed again.

"Good try," he says, "but you clearly got your coordination skills from your mother. Let me get it for you. We'll be here all night if we let you do it."

Just like he promised, Dad got me the fish. Unfortunately, my plan to win it using as few tickets as possible was a miserable failure, but he did it, and that's what counts, because that's where I think he's right and Mom's wrong. I know I don't *need* the fish like he said, but I do like that he wanted to win it for me. It's his way of making me happy. And if he thinks that winning me this lump of fish-shaped rainbow fluff is what makes me happy —

and it makes him happy to think that — then as far as I'm concerned, it's money well spent. So now, just like last year and the year before, the three of us are sitting in the grandstand with two huge unnecessary but necessary stuffed things wedged between us, watching the cars get into position for the derby.

The derby is Dad and Jonah's most favorite thing at the fair. Like Dad says, what's not to love about a bunch of cars smashing into each other in a mud-filled pit? I like it for different reasons. It's at the time of day between light and dark when the fairground's twinkly lights sparkle, and the heat of the day is carried off with the cool breeze of the evening. It's the time I get to sit and relax. I was hoping that this year we might at least make it to the horse show or the Around the World exhibit like we used to with Mom, but Dad didn't seem interested when I suggested it, and I didn't want to make an issue about it. I tell myself it's better this way, that it's easier to just go along with what Dad wants to do.

I steal a sideways glance at him. I still haven't mentioned Sunridge. I dig my fingernails into my palms, simultaneously punishing myself for my cowardice while also urging myself to just do it already.

"Hey, Lexie," says Dad, jarring me from the argument I'm having with myself. "We could use some cotton candy, don't you think?"

"Yeah," says Jonah, stretching his neck out to talk to me around Dad. "And some caramel corn."

Dad pulls his much smaller roll of money from his pocket and peels a twenty from it. I take it, and can't help but notice how the deep purple crescent shapes that my nails cut into the soft flesh of my palms smile obscenely at me.

"Sure. Good idea."

I pocket his money and walk away from them, letting my nose lead me to the sugar shack while I rub furiously at the mocking smiles, try to make them and what they represent disappear.

I won't ruin this day. I'll tell him tomorrow.

CHAPTER FOUR

SUNDAY, OCTOBER 22

The elevator moans with its usual protest as it jerks its way to the fifth floor. I plant my feet far apart, knees bent, and stand like a ninja trying to hold my balance between the three cans of paint we just bought and Dad's Rubbermaid tub of painting supplies. I refuse to touch anything in here, and stick to mouth breathing only. Every surface is covered in a layer of grime and graffiti, and the air is thick and sticky, like chowder soup. It smells like a whole lot of people have been cooking sweaty sport socks in stale, curried cooking oil for a few years too many, and I learned the hard way that if I breathe it in, the stink will cling in my nostrils for hours.

I thought I was done with this place. When I agreed to help a few weeks ago, it was a quick extra job, not this permanent new job. Jonah and I have spent the last few weekends here, helping Dad fix up a couple of units on the fourth floor. It was a job Dad picked up from a guy he knows to make some extra money. I was happy to help him, especially when he said he'd give us a cut. The work was easy — nothing we hadn't helped

Dad with before. As usual, Jonah helped Dad with the grunt work — tearing stuff out and hammering stuff back in. If he wasn't hitting, sawing, or building something, he wasn't happy. I was happy to let him do it — not because I can't do the grunt work (thanks to Dad, I know my way around the tools of a home renovation), but because I prefer the work that requires a careful hand. That's the part of the project that necessitates working slowly and methodically, like how I like to approach a new sketch or painting. I know most people would think it's nuts that I like helping my dad with work like this, but it's actually fun. I bring my speakers and blast Taylor Swift and Gracie Abrams just loud enough to make Jonah complain. Dad complains too, but it's just a show for Jonah. I know because I've caught him singing along with me, even though he denies it. Even so, when I finished painting the last of the doorjambs and caulking around the new sinks and tubs that Dad and Jonah installed last weekend, I was happy to be done. Three weekends in a row helping Dad was enough for me, especially given the amount of homework I had piling up. That's why I couldn't hide my annoyed surprise when he told us that he needed our help here again today.

"He hired you to do another six units?" I heard my voice squeak upward, praying he didn't notice.

A whisk of a proud smile flashed across his lips. "He liked the work I did on those other two units so much, he wants me to reno the entire fifth floor."

My brain raced around, trying to figure out the logistics of it all. I didn't want to ask how he'd manage this job around his regular job — I knew better than that — but I needed to know. "But when will you have time?"

He waved his hand, like he was shooing away an annoying insect. "I quit the dealership, so time's not an issue."

My stomach tugged. How were we going to pay the rent?

"But no one needs to know that, right?" His grin turned smug, perching precariously on his lips like it might fall off.

I nodded, assuring him that I wouldn't tell Mom. He knew he could trust me and my silence. If I was one thing, I was reliable. I wouldn't tell her anyway. Experience has taught me that telling her stuff like this just makes it harder for Jonah and me. It's better that she doesn't know. At least that's what Dad says, and I'm pretty sure he's right.

He continued. "I decided to start a family renovation business. Jonah's all in. Right, Jonah?"

Jonah's head bobbed up and down like a ball atop a spring. Then Dad fixed his gaze on me. I knew the look well: It was the one he laid on you when there was only one acceptable answer to whatever his question was.

"You're in too, right? Because no one paints better and pays attention to the tiny details better than you." He tilted his head to his shoulder. "It's probably all those art classes you've taken. They've paid off."

His eyes radiated with pride and I couldn't contain the smile that quivered at the corners of my lips. His approval of my skill set — and telling me it was valuable to his success — was enough for me to shove the growing list of worries to the back of my mind.

"I guess I can help out sometimes. Just not all —"

"And me quitting saves you time. I don't have to suck up to Blakeman anymore, so you can quit going to the nursing home."

Dad's boss, Norm Blakeman, was married to Valerie Blakeman, the volunteer coordinator at the nursing home. Dad had thought me volunteering there would impress his boss.

"But I like going there —"

"Because of Mr. Harris?" asked Dad. "That old man fills your head with crazy ideas."

There was no point in arguing. I'd figure out a way of helping Dad and visiting Mr. Harris. I was an expert at making everyone happy. "I knew I could count on you," said Dad. "The three of us are going to turn this into a great family business."

My words piled up in my throat like useless bricks, sealing off my ability to say what needed to be said. I know I need to clarify that I could only help sometimes, and not the way I'm pretty sure he expects me to, but I couldn't disappoint him. I'll just help him get it started. That can't be too much work. Like he said, I'm the only one who pays attention to the details, so it would be inconsiderate of me to not help. He needs me. I can't forget what's most important.

A lethargic ding signals my arrival on the fifth floor. The elevator grinds to a shaking stop and the door yawns open. Pressing my left foot against the doorframe, I drag the painting supplies into the hallway, and then half drag, half carry everything to unit 506. A fresh wave of garbage-tinged stink greets me when I use the keys Dad gave me to open the door. I pull my shirt up over my nose and let my eyes take in the space from the safety of the hallway. A filthy, ripped sofa piled with broken furniture and bags of garbage sits in the middle of the living area, a stained mattress propped up against its side. The kitchen to the left is no better, its counters piled with what I assume are the contents of the cupboards, which stand with their flimsy doors hanging open, empty. Another pile of garbage bags sits in front of the sink, doing nothing to hide the yellowed linoleum flooring that's cracked and peeling where it meets the worn brown carpeting of the living room. A quick peek around the corner reveals the bathroom and a whole other level of disgusting, and I regret agreeing to help again. (I didn't have much choice, but I tell myself that I did.)

The elevator groans from down the hall, announcing Dad and Jonah's arrival.

"So, what do you think?" Dad asks, stepping around me, surveying the space.

I don't answer him, careful not to say anything that might lead him to think I want to be here. Instead, I stuff my nose back in my shirt, grab a garbage bag from the couch in each hand, and head back down the stink-filled elevator to find the dumpster, cursing myself for not telling him about Sunridge yesterday because it's clear that finding a good time to tell him today isn't going to happen.

CHAPTER FIVE

MONDAY, OCTOBER 23

Dad started looking green about an hour after we got home from the job site last night. I made him as comfortable as I could on the couch with his pillow and blanket, and gave him the last of the Gravol I found in the medicine cabinet. I don't know that it helped him much, though, because I heard him in and out of the bathroom most of the night. Needless to say, I didn't get much sleep. I don't think it was just him, though. I had a lot on my mind, like today's chem test, my portfolio, swim practice, the fact that I'm overdue for a visit with Mr. Harris at the nursing home, and of course, now everything that's involved in planning a spring regatta. Nate was all over the idea as I knew he would be. Boats and duct tape are two of his most favorite things. We'll need Zara's help if we're going to pull it off. Between her work with the dog rescue she volunteers with, her charity work for the MS Foundation, and her position on student council, she's always in the midst of planning something.

I look at Dad, passed out on the couch, his arm dangling over the side, the bucket I left on the floor beside him, and my stomach does its sickening floppy thing. I still haven't brought up Sunridge, and now I've run out of time to talk to him. Again.

His eyes flutter open when I put his breakfast of dry toast and coffee on the table beside him. His face is a pasty shade of grayish white.

"You all right?" I ask him, clearing the coffee table of the pile of dirty dishes that always seem to accumulate on it.

He moans, clutching his stomach. "No. Can you get me some more Gravol?"

"It's all gone. I gave you the last of it last night."

He struggles to sit up. "Can you walk to the pharmacy and get some more? And maybe some soup and ginger ale?"

He pulls a fifty from the much smaller roll of cash in his pocket and hands it to me. I take it, but my eyes flicker to the clock over the fridge. There's no way I can go to the pharmacy and not be late for my first period chem test.

He must know what I'm thinking because he says, "Why don't you stay home today? I need someone to take care of me."

My mind spins as I try to figure out how to make it work. Now that I know how to draw Lewis dot diagrams, I'd like to get my test over with. But on the other hand, staying home will give me time alone with him, to tell him what I need to tell him. There's also the fact that if I say no, he'll ask Jonah to do it and then it'll be all about how Jonah cares more about him than I do. I can't deal with that. And I know Mr. Ellis will let me write the test tomorrow over lunch if I miss it today, so the test isn't an issue. The biggest issue will be Mom.

Dad senses my hesitation. "What? You don't want to stay home with me?"

"Of course I do. But I have a chemistry test today."

His frown melts away and he rolls his eyes. "You taking care of your dad is way more important than that. It's just a test. It doesn't mean anything."

My lips press together. I don't argue. It's not worth it. Instead I say, "Mom won't like it."

He scoffs. "She doesn't need to know."

"Yes, she does. Remember what happened last time?"

A look of irritation crosses his eyes. "Fine. But you know how much of a control freak she is. She's not going to want you to spend time with me."

I nod, even though I know Mom's issue will be more about me missing school than about spending time with him, but I don't correct him. I'm never going to change his mind about that.

I text her as I walk to the pharmacy. I've barely hit send when she calls.

"What do you mean you're staying home?" Her voice is controlled, but disapproval wraps her words.

"Dad's sick. He was up all night."

I hear her sigh through the phone, and I know what she looks like, sitting with her elbows on the kitchen table, her thumb and index finger shaped like a V, rubbing her forehead.

"Lexie, your dad can take care of himself. You have a test today."

"I can write it tomorrow. It's not a big deal."

Her voice gets hard. "Lexie. No. You need to get to school."

Whoa.

Anger builds inside me, not unlike the storm clouds brewing above. She doesn't get it. She doesn't understand why I need this day and I'm not going to explain it to her. I grip the phone tighter.

"This isn't your call. Dad asked me to stay home and I'm going to. I'm letting you know so you don't freak out like you did the last time I missed a day."

The silence on the line is thick. I don't have to see her to know that her lips are pressed into a thin line, the lines around her eyes tight.

"Fine. But this better not become a habit."

"It won't," I say. "I promise. It's just one day."

CHAPTER SIX

THURSDAY, OCTOBER 26

I know something's up when I get home from school and find Zara sitting on our front porch, her knee bouncing.

"Don't you answer your messages?"

"My phone died and I forgot my charger," I say. "What's up?"

Her stare is pointy, like she's trying to see inside my brain. "Did you forget you had something to do yesterday?"

I think back to the day before, which was the same as the three days before that, which was Dad, Jonah, and me working in the apartment building.

"I don't think so."

"So you did forget!"

I give her a blank look. I've got nothing left.

"Your *date* with Hot Lifeguard." She emphasizes the *d* and *t* in date. "You were supposed to meet him at the pool last night, after swim practice, which you also missed."

My stomach drops into my feet. I had completely lost track of the days. I was thinking that was tonight. *Crap! No, no, no, no, no!*

"How do I fix this?"

The corner of her mouth twitches.

"What?" I ask.

"Well, after you stood him up —"

Argh! Not on purpose!

"— he asked one of his friends if they knew you, who said no, but they knew you were friends with me, so then they asked Jenna, who knew my friend Libby from student council, who texted me today to tell me that Rhys wanted your number."

My heart flops around, like a fish in the bottom of a boat.

"I didn't get her message right away, though, because I was stuck in phys ed. When I got it, I texted you like six times, but you IGNORED ME."

"I didn't. My phone was dead!"

"So I decided that you'd be okay with me passing Libby your number to pass to Rhys."

"So he has my number? You're not joking?"

"Don't be dumb, Lexie. This isn't something I'd joke about."

Okay. Fair enough.

"How long ago did this happen?" I ask.

She shrugs. "About five hours ago."

I want to kick myself with pointy boots. I can't believe I missed what could've been the best night of my life.

"Do you think he's actually going to call?"

She tilts her head and gives me her that's-the-stupidest-thing-you've-ever-said look. "No guy goes to that much trouble to get a girl's number and then doesn't call. In fact, maybe he already did and you have no idea because YOUR PHONE IS STILL DEAD."

With Zara on my heels, we take the stairs two at a time up to my room. I plug in my phone and it starts pinging with message after message. They're all from Zara except one that's from Dad telling me that he needs my help again tomorrow. Nothing from Rhys.

"He's going to call. I just know it," she says.

A beat of silence goes by while we both stare at my phone, willing it to ring.

"I guess I just have to wait," I say.

She shrugs. "Not much else you can do."

He texts at ten o'clock. I cross my room in two strides and dive to the bottom of my laundry bin to get my phone. I'd stuffed it there two hours ago so I could concentrate on my homework rather than wonder why it was taking him so long to text me, when he's had my number for hours. My heart skips a beat when I read his message.

Hey. It's Rhys. Missed you last night. Got your number from a friend. Want to try again next week?

YES!

My fingers type fast.

Sorry I missed you! Yes, next week!

My thumb hovers over the send button, but I read it again, and I sound like a desperate idiot. I also realize that if I text back too fast, I'll look like an even bigger desperate idiot. I erase my response and tear a piece of paper from my binder. I write out a few possible ways to respond:

1. Sorry, I was sick. (white lie) Yes for next week (thumbs-up emoji)
2. Sorry, I was sick. Would love to try again next week! (smiley face emoji)
3. Sorry, I was sick. Yes for next week (smiley face emoji)

I go with option three. The thumbs-up emoji makes me seem dorky (or does it?), and option two still makes me sound desperate. I type it into my phone and proofread it three times before I hit send. He responds right away:

Great. C u there 👍

Huh. I guess it's not as dorky as I thought.

CHAPTER SEVEN

SATURDAY, OCTOBER 28

Even though I can't see around the back of the marina, the fact that I can smell sawdust, motor oil, and varnish, and hear the crooning, mellow sound of Kings of Leon, tells me the marina's shop door is open and Nate's already busy working. He messaged yesterday, asking if Zara and I could come. He said he was ready to get back at it, and could we help him clean up and organize the marina? I knew it was code for "I don't want to go through Pops's things by myself," and to be honest, I feel the same way. Pops's absence is still too heavy for me to deal with alone.

I let Zara go ahead of me carrying the platter of her mom's famous shish tawook and pita, with a box of gluten-free crackers she sent special for me, while I stop at the mailbox. As I expected, it's stuffed. I'm not sure if they haven't collected it because they're not used to doing it, as it was something that Pops always did, or if they're avoiding it because they're afraid of the pile of bills they might find. My guess is the latter.

Nate's back is to me when I duck under the half-open rusted shop door. Zara's watching Nate, who is bent over a 15 hp outboard motor that a customer dropped off for repair.

"Need a break?" I ask, loud enough that he can hear me over the music. "Zara's mom sent food."

He turns at the sound of my voice and wipes his hands on an old towel. His eyes rake over the platter Zara's balancing on her hip.

"Definitely. Did you bring her tahini-garlic sauce too?"

Zara gives him her well-duh look. Nate takes the platter from her and puts it on the overturned crates we use as a coffee table. He plops himself into the folding metal lawn chair next to it while Zara and I perch on Gertrude, which is our name for the ugly couch — or as Pops called it, a chesterfield. It's the only place of reasonable comfort to sit. (I use the term comfort loosely.) Gertrude's ancient. Her ornate wood frame is perched atop four curved wooden legs, her arms as high as her back, and she's been repaired with duct tape in more than a few places. The duct tape does nothing to hide the offensive olive-green flower pattern that's stitched into the worn yellow velour covering her cushions and scalloped back.

Zara hands us each a paper plate loaded with a skewer of chicken, a few triangles of pita (crackers for me), lettuce, dill pickles, and pickled turnip, and of course, a generous dollop of sauce.

"Now eat," she commands us both just as her phone chirps from the depths of her bag. She pulls it out and squeals with delight. "Guys," she says, "you have to see this one." She turns her phone to show us a photo of a long-haired black dog with a tuft of white hair on his chest. "His name's Maverick. Our newest rescue. Isn't he just adorable?"

I trade a glance with Nate. Zara's always trying to get Nate and me to convince our parents to adopt one of the dogs the rescue brings in, and I always explain to her that while I'd love to, neither of my parents can afford a dog. Never mind the fact that I have zero time for a dog. Nate's told her the same thing.

"He's about four months old," she continues, "and just the sweetest thing." She jiggles her phone from side to side, her hopeful gaze sliding back and forth between us.

Nate blows out a breath. "I wish we could, Zara, but we can't. Especially right now."

Zara skewers me with her gaze. I lift my shoulder. "For all the reasons I've already told you, my parents can't either. Sorry."

She sighs. "It was worth a shot." She shoves her phone back in her bag. "Your brother, though, was all over him."

"Jonah?"

"Yeah. He and his friends were at Duey's Dips when Debbie brought him in." Debbie is the manager of the rescue. "He said he was going to beg your dad to adopt him."

I roll my eyes. "He always does that. Doesn't change reality though."

Nate holds out his plate to Zara, wordlessly requesting a second skewer. She dumps one on his plate.

"Did you get my text about helping us organize a regatta?" he asks.

She nods and wipes sauce from the corner of her mouth with her thumb. "It sounds like a great idea, and totally doable. Boat races, some food trucks, some carnival games." Her voice trails off and her eyes go to the ceiling. "But we'll need to get a permit from the city first. Then we can get the word out through my Instagram and put flyers up at the rec center, and we should list all the details on the marina's website. You guys have a website, don't you? We're going to have to get people to register if they want to race, otherwise it'll be an organizational nightmare."

She reaches into her bag for her day planner, highlighter, and colored clicky pen, three things she never leaves home without. She opens the day planner to a fresh page and looks at Nate.

"I need to make a chart of all the things we need to do. You got a ruler?"

He gets up and gets one from the drawer in the workbench.

"Thanks. I just hate it when my lines aren't straight."

My eyes find Nate's, and he nods. We both know that Zara's crazy is about to be let loose. It's no joke. Once Zara decides to take on projects like this, she jumps in with both feet and doesn't look back. There's no stopping her.

"So, in terms of boats," she says. "Will it be canoes and kayaks, or were you expecting that people would bring their own motorboats? Because if you're thinking motorboats, that'll be a lot more difficult to —"

"You didn't tell her about the boats?" I ask Nate.

"I might not have included that tiny detail."

"What detail?" Zara asks, sliding her pen along the ruler's edge.

"That the boats will be homemade," I say.

Her pen freezes, hovering over her notepad. Her head stays frozen in place but her eyes peer up through her thick, mascaraed lashes. "I'm sorry, what?"

"We were hoping to attract even more people by inviting them to build their own boats," Nate says. "Out of cardboard and duct tape."

There's a pause as her eyes slide back and forth between us. "You want to make boats out of paper and tape?"

I press my lips together, suppressing a laugh.

"Isn't it brilliant?" Nate pulls a piece of paper from his pocket and smooths it out on his thigh. "I've already sketched out some ideas. Which of these boats do you see yourselves in? Should I build us the Yellow Bananarama, Gorgeous Gertrude, or Turbo Turtle? I'm proud of Turbo Turtle myself, but I'm open to suggestions."

Zara looks at him like he's got a screw loose.

"My vote's with Gorgeous Gertrude," I say, patting Gertrude's cushion. "Paddling across the lake on a floating cardboard version of this old girl will be the most brilliant thing ever."

"Okay," Nate says, "but that's also the one that will be the most difficult, designwise."

"I think it's worth the risk," I say.

"I don't think sending scores of people out onto a lake in paper boats screams of brilliance," Zara says.

"Cardboard, not paper," says Nate.

"Cardboard *is* paper," she says.

"It's way more sturdy than paper. Even more when you wrap it up with duct tape, the greatest invention ever."

I laugh out loud.

"I will not be setting a single toe in any one of those harebrained death traps," Zara says. "I'll stick to organizing the logistics, thanks."

Nate rolls his eyes. "Fine. But I'll bet you that if this goes well, it could be the first of many regattas we host, and one way or another, you're going to get in one."

She shakes her head, a firm never-not-ever-going-to-happen.

Nate smiles a smile that says he thinks he's already won, and pops the last of his third chicken skewer in his mouth. "We'll see about that."

After polishing off the platter of food, and then the date-filled ma'amoul cookies that Zara's mom also sent, we busy ourselves for the rest of the day, organizing and cleaning everything everywhere. I knew that Pops didn't like to throw things away, but I didn't realize the extent of it. We clean off shelves jammed with empty cans of sealant, and half-full cans of paint, and tubs filled with assorted nails and screws. We empty and refill drawers stuffed with loose drill bits and wood screws, batteries, rolls of tape, and twenty-year-old receipts for two-dollar bottles of glue. We clean off the workbench, hang tools back in their proper place on the pegboard, return power tools to the tool cabinet, empty the bins stored underneath the workbench, file defunct engine parts and offcuts of wood in the garbage, and untangle and hang masses of rope and extension cords.

Nate and I are more than ready to call it a day when Zara decides to climb the ladder to assess the stuff stored in racks above the workbench. Nate groans and rubs the back of his neck.

"Zara, aren't you tired?"

"Nope. And you're not allowed to be either. Not until we finish what we started."

He grumbles at her, but doesn't argue. Zara struggles under the weight of a box labeled "CWP." "What does 'CWP' stand for?"

Nate takes it from her, placing it on the workbench. Inside are piles of file folders, stacked on end, lined up one after another, each one labeled, each one stuffed with paper, some more than others.

"It means crossword puzzles," I say, my voice quiet, when Nate doesn't answer. "Pops was really into crossword puzzles — not just doing them, but creating his own. But I had no idea he made this many of them."

I pull a folder labeled "Around the World" from the middle of the box and flip it open. At the top of each page, in Pops's neat block script, is the title of each puzzle. There's "Bodies of Water," "Cities in Egypt," "The Beaches of Fiji," and "Birds of Guanacaste, Costa Rica" to name just a few. All of them are hand drawn.

"Did you know he had this many?" I ask Nate, ache ballooning in my throat.

Nate takes the folder from me. "I knew," he says, his voice filled with regret. "I told him I'd help him get them organized and figure out the next step, but I got so busy doing repairs around here, and then finishing the courses I needed to get my mechanic's license, that I just never got around to it."

"What do you mean, next step?" Zara asks.

"He wanted to publish them," Nate says. "He wanted to be a published cruciverbalist."

"Cruci-what?"

"Cruciverbalist. A writer of crossword puzzles. He was convinced his puzzles would get published in *The New York Times*, and that he'd make enough money to pay off some of our bills." He flips through another folder labeled "Domesticated Animals." "Maybe he wasn't wrong."

Then he shoves the folder back in the box, and rams the lid back on, closing the lid on his grief.

Despite turning off my light forty-five minutes ago, I'm still awake. I know it's because of Pops's puzzles. I can't stop thinking about them. Throwing off my covers, I switch my lamp back on and open the folder I slipped into my bag when Nate wasn't looking. Again, I'm amazed at the detail and research that must have gone into creating them.

Grabbing my phone, I type "crossword puzzle publisher" into Google's search bar. A website listing a bunch of places to submit puzzles to pops up. I suck in a breath when I see that one of the first on the list is *The New York Times*. The seeds of a plan start to take shape in my mind. I'll figure out what needs to be done to make Pops's dream come true so that when Nate's ready, everything will be all teed up for him.

I bookmark the website and turn off my phone, unable to contain the smile that's now stuck on my face. Then I switch off the light and I'm asleep within minutes.

CHAPTER EIGHT

WEDNESDAY, NOVEMBER 1

I drop my towel and swim bag on the bleachers that line the length of the pool. Except for an older couple swimming laps in lanes one and two, the pool's empty. I glance at the clock above the change room doors. 7:53. I tell myself that it's early. That it's reasonable he's not here yet. That it doesn't mean he's not coming. I haven't heard anything from him since we rescheduled our swim. Is it weird that he hasn't texted? Does it mean he's changed his mind?

Earlier today, I asked Zara what she thought, and she told me that no guy would have gone to the trouble of tracking down my number to reschedule a date only to not show up. "That'd be dumb," I think were her exact words. "If you're so worried, why don't you ask him?"

"Text to ask if he's still coming?"

"Yeah. Or you could say something like, 'Looking forward to tonight.' That way he knows you're still planning to go, and he can say that he is too. Or, you could ask if eight o'clock still works. That way it just seems like you're trying to plan, and not that you're, like, being pushy."

"You think if I text him he might think I'm pushy?"

"Holy crap, Lexie."

Needless to say, I didn't text him. I figured I'd just show up and hopefully he would too. I sit on the bleachers to wait. My butterflies have been flapping about all day in anticipation of seeing him, like they've been rehearsing for a performance of *The Nutcracker*. My hands are a bit clammy too, which is gross. I wipe them on my thighs. I glance at the clock again. 7:57. What should I do? Keep sitting here or get in the pool? Getting in the pool will help calm my crazy, and I'll look like less of a dork than if I'm just sitting here waiting.

I assume my position on the block, feel its roughness under my feet, and press my goggles to my eyes. Then I shake out my arms and legs before I dive off, slicing through the water's surface with my fingertips. The gurgle of the broken stillness fills my ears, and I slip into my zone and move with the rhythm that the fly demands. It takes me about half a length to find it, but when I do, I slide into the motion and don't even have to think about it. I know I'm not breaking any records, but I know my form's good. It's like my body's woken up to what it's supposed to do. I'm coming to the end of my fourth length when I notice him standing next to the bleachers, peeling off his workout suit. His abs stretch out as he pulls his shirt over his head and my butterflies crash into the walls of my stomach.

"What the heck? Last week you were no-show, and this week you start without me?"

My blood scrambles into a mess and heat rises up the back of my neck, making my scalp prickle. I open my mouth to defend myself but no words come out. It's then that I notice the smile playing at the corners of his mouth.

"I'm kidding. My band practice ran late. Of course it's okay that you started. It'd be weird if you were just sitting waiting, wouldn't it?"

I glance down at the water, certain that the hooves of the two thousand wild horses galloping through my chest are making ripples in the water. I'm relieved to see I'm wrong. I swallow, give myself a few seconds for my body to put itself back together.

"That's what I figured. Sorry again about last week. I was sick."

He grins, showcasing his solo left dimple that I didn't notice before, and slips into the pool beside me.

"That's all right. I figured something must've come up. I'm just glad you're here now."

He's so close to me, I can't help but stare into the blue sapphires that are his eyes. I've never seen anyone with eyes quite that color.

"Should we get it on?" he says.

Holy crap, what?

"What?"

"I meant swim. Want to swim?"

"Oh. Yeah."

He smiles, showing off his perfect dimple. "Great. Race you."

"That was a good practice. Your form's looking better already," he says as we set out on the footpath toward my house.

I told him that he didn't need to walk me home, that it wasn't far and the path was well lit, but he insisted, and secretly, I was pleased.

As we walk, I can't help noticing how close he walks to me, and how his hand keeps knocking into mine, like he's trying to hook my finger with his, but can't quite decide if he should or not. I don't do much breathing, so it's a good thing it's only a few minutes' walk, or I might have passed out. But then again, maybe that wouldn't have been a bad thing, because he likely would've tried to perform mouth-to-mouth on me, being a lifeguard and all. I consider what it would be like if such a scenario happened, and I'm so caught up in the fantasy that I lose track of what he's saying.

"I submitted it last night."

"Submitted what?"

"An application to that program at Sunridge. The one you applied to."

"Oh! That's great."

"Some other people I know also applied, so I decided to go for it. Keep my options open. Won't hurt anyone to try, right?"

He slows on the path and steps in front of me so that he's facing me.

"Besides, the added bonus is that you'll be there."

I feel my face get hot, and I'm glad it's dark because I'm pretty sure I'm as red as a fire-roasted tomato.

"I hope I'll be there," I say.

But you won't be if you don't hurry up and tell Dad so you can submit the application.

He's so close I can feel his heat, smell the lingering scent of his soap from his post-swim shower. It's both woodsy and spicy at the same time. His still-wet hair seems to have a mind of its own, the way it curls around his earlobes, and I can't help thinking that he could make bedhead look hot. I resist the urge to brush the hair that's flopped over his forehead out of his eyes.

"I haven't been able to stop thinking about you," he says.

I know I should say something, but my heart's a pitter-pattery mess. I feel like I've tricked him into thinking I'm someone I'm not, because this can't be happening to me. I'm nothing like those cheerleader girls that guys like him go for, with their perfect hair and makeup, shoes that match their shirts. I feel like I should tell him that he's wrong about me, that I'm not who he thinks I am, but I don't because I don't want to.

He widens his stance, brings his face closer to mine, tucks a loose strand of hair behind my ear. My breath catches, and the herd of wild horses is back, trampling all over my insides. My eyes lock on his. His breath is warm on my cheek, and then his lips brush against mine, in a barely-there-I-don't-even-know-if-it's-a-kiss kiss, before he pulls away, leaving a tingly feeling on my lips, like tiny bubbles popping, and it feels like maybe I'm living someone else's life. It's a feeling I want to hold on to forever, and I forget that I'm just regular me, and I let myself be who I think he wants me to be.

"Sorry. Was that okay?" he asks.

"Yeah," I croak out. "Totally okay."

And then my lips meet his again. When he pulls away, I'm unable to tear my eyes from his.

"When can I see you again? Tomorrow? Same place?"

Of course, Zara couldn't wait to hear about the date. I told her I'd call her when I got home, but she's not good at waiting. I've scarcely made it home and past Mom's regular "how was your swim" line of questioning when she texts three times in a span of two minutes.

U home yet?
Helloooo?
How'd it go? DETAILS!!

I put her out of her misery and FaceTime her. I tell her that he tried to help me work on the rhythm of my stroke, but all I could see was how awesome his shoulders looked as they rolled forward in the water, how the water rushed over them with every stroke. "And then he kissed me."

Her hands slap her cheeks. "Holy Hannah, no he didn't."

I struggle to keep a straight face. I use one of her own lines against her: "This isn't something I'd joke about."

Two parallel lines cut the space between her eyebrows. "Isn't that a bit fast for a first date? What kind of kiss was it? Was it like a peck or was there tongue involved? Are you sure you know what you're doing?"

I think of his kiss, and how light, airy butterflies tickled my insides. I may not know what I'm doing, but I'm definitely okay with seeing what happens next.

"There was no tongue, as you so grossly put it, and I was fine with it. And it just kind of happened. It's not like you think. He's not like that."

"If you say so," she says. "Just —"

"Just what?"

"Don't do anything you don't want to do."

"Of course I won't."

"Good. I just want to make sure he isn't trying to get into your pants."

"Zara!"

"Hey. I wouldn't be a good BFF if I didn't say it. You'll do the same for me when I'm thirty and my parents finally let me date."

I laugh out loud. "Now you're exaggerating."

She gives me one of her looks. "You have met my parents, haven't you?"

I fall asleep staring at my ceiling, wondering what I've done to land such a hot guy. Whatever it is, I'm not about to let anyone screw it up for me. I'm ready to step outside of my comfort zone and take a risk. Prove to him and myself that I can be an awesome girlfriend. It can't be too hard. I'm used to pretending to be someone I'm not. I do it with Dad all the time. If anyone can make this work, it's me.

CHAPTER NINE

TUESDAY, NOVEMBER 7

I hear the hiss of Mr. Harris's oxygen tank before I see him. The tubing, normally coiled on the hook of the trolley the tank sits in, spills out into a pile on the floor beside him. He's sitting at the small table in the corner of his room, the Scrabble board already set up, waiting for me, his lunch dishes pushed to the side. I tap on his door.

"How are you today, Mr. Harris?"

He grunts. "I'd be better if the girl who's supposed to play Scrabble with me at four o'clock showed up on time."

I don't let him see my smile. I don't buy his grouchy act for a second. I've been visiting him long enough to know that it's not real. It's four minutes after four. If I'm not ten minutes early, he thinks I'm late. It does scare some of the new personal support workers though, which I'm betting is why his lunch dishes haven't been cleared away yet. He probably chastised one of them for helping the wrong way, so they forgot to come back to his room. I gather the dishes onto his tray and carry them out into the hall, putting them on the cart.

"Did you get your coffee?" I ask, picking up the tubing and placing it back on its hook.

"No. They forgot again. They always forget."

"Do you want me to get it for you? Black with two sugars, right?"

"No. If I've told you once, I've told you a thousand times. I don't want you to clean up my room or bring me coffee. They have staff here to do that."

The way he says it makes me hesitate. It's nothing I haven't heard before, but this time it's different, like he means it.

"Scrabble it is, then," I say, sliding into the chair opposite him.

A breeze blows through his open window, the curtain catching his plant. A dried leaf falls and skitters across the floor, under our table. I steal a quick glance at him, knowing what he's going to say.

"At least cut the dead branches off the wretched thing," he says, his eyes trained on the board.

"There aren't any dead branches, Mr. Harris," I say.

He shakes his head, like he can't believe he has to explain it to me again. "Well, that's your problem. You refuse to see the evidence in front of you. Those dead branches are what's keeping that plant from thriving."

I ignore him, study my tiles. Two *E*'s, an *O*, a *Y*, a *Q*, an *R*, and one *B*. Great.

"I'm sorry I made you wait. My English teacher had more to say than any of us wanted to hear about how Lady Macbeth used language to manipulate Macbeth, which made me miss my regular bus. I didn't forget about our date."

His gaze softens, and I see the real Mr. Harris show himself. The one whose eyes light up when he sees me, even though he doesn't know and would hate it if he knew that his eyes gave him away.

"Maybe you should tell your English teacher that he should be more respectful of time," he says. "There's more to life than his class."

I nod. "Maybe I should."

I definitely shouldn't.

He turns his focus back to his tiles.

"Did you apply to Sunridge yet? You said applications were due in the fall. Last time I checked, it was fall."

My stomach twists, like someone turns a screw in it, and it reminds me that I'm running out of time. I told Mom that I told Dad, just to get her off my case. She asked if he was okay with it, with one eyebrow raised, and I lied and told her he was, and changed the subject. I'm pretty sure she didn't believe me.

"Not yet," I say.

"What's the hold up?"

I shrug, hoping he'll drop the subject.

"It's a lot of money, and my dad ..."

I let my voice trail off, hoping he'll let it go, but his eyes are locked on mine, waiting for an explanation.

"He's not convinced I should go."

He scowls, looks at me like I just suggested we play checkers instead of Scrabble. "Why on earth would he need convincing?"

Heat rises in me, spreading like fire, and I keep my eyes trained on my tiles. Silence punctuates the space between us and I feel his eyes burning a hole in the top of my head. I shrug again, hoping it'll shrug off his interest. Finally, I feel his eyes shift away from me back to the board, and I can breathe again. He lays the word *EXETER* on the board.

"That's quite the word. What's it mean?"

"It's a city. In England."

"Is that allowed?"

"Don't you think I know the rules?"

"I was just checking," I say, pleased that we're back to our usual Scrabble banter.

"Talk to your dad," Mr. Harris says. I feel his gaze on me again, but this time it's less razor-sharp, like it's laced with concern, or maybe pity.

"I'm sorry?"

"He needs to know how important this is to you. Promise me you'll apply to Sunridge."

My eyes drift down to the Scrabble board. I rearrange my tiles.

"You owe me a promise."

I look at him. "A promise?"

He waves his hand at his plant. "You made me promise not to get rid of that half-dead stump of a plant, so you owe me a promise too."

I glance at it, out of the corner of my eye. It does look past its due date, but I'm not admitting that to him. It's half the size it was when I first met him, all its bright purple blooms long gone. I've been trying to resurrect it for months now, with no luck. I made him promise not to throw it out, to let me work my magic. I'm hoping I'll have better luck than I've been having with my ferns. He has kept his promise, although not without complaining about it pretty much every time I visit.

I nod, understanding by the earnest look in his eye that he's very serious, and that me following through on my plans to apply to Sunridge is, for some reason, important to him.

"Okay, Mr. Harris. I promise."

He sits back then, satisfied. "Good. Now play your word."

I lay down *TREE* using the *T* in *EXETER*.

He snorts. "Is that the best you got?"

"My letter selection is somewhat lacking," I say.

I choose three more tiles from the bag to replace the *R* and two *E*'s I just used and arrange them on my tile stand. I get a *V*, an *M*, and a *W*. Friggin' fantastic.

"It's interesting, don't you think, how you always set up the game before I get here, and you somehow always have all the letter tiles you need to lay down a high-scoring first word?"

His face pinches together with a furious look. "I'm going to take that to mean that you're jealous of my linguistic talent, and that you're not at all suggesting that I'm cheating."

"Of course," I say. "I was just making an observation. What was the word you put down last week? 'Quiz' something?"

He flips through the little notebook he keeps with the game board. Over the two and a half years that I've been playing with him, he's kept a record of every word we've played, and every point we've scored, in that little blue book.

"It was *QUIZZER*, with one *Z* a blank and the other on a double-letter tile. And then you placed *RICE*, using the *R* in *QUIZZER*."

I nod. "I remember now."

I study the board again. Darn it. He's won again, and we've just started. He's used the *X* in *EXETER* to spell *EXPEL*.

I lay down *BOWL* using the *L* in *EXPEL*. It's all I've got.

He grunts. "It's not looking good for you, girlie. I think I'm going to kick your butt again."

CHAPTER TEN

THURSDAY, NOVEMBER 16

I'm sitting in my usual spot on the loveseat in Dr. Crowchild's office, where I have a full view of the large bay window, its deep sill filled with a variety of perennials, succulents, and exotic plants that all look like they could be featured in *Plantlife* magazine. A basket of perennials dominates the center of the window; their tall, waxy leaves, ranging from lime green to a deep shade of plum, stretch high, reaching for the feathers that hang from the dream catcher dangling above them. Small red and yellow flowers and a trail of ivy spill out of the basket beneath them, and a tiny model of the medicine wheel on a spike adorns the center of the arrangement.

I can't help admiring them. Doesn't seem to matter what I do, plants hate me. I've already replaced the fern in my room twice, and it seems Mr. Harris's plant likes me about the same as the ferns do. Not replacing that one, though. Especially not after he promised he'd keep it. I wonder what Dr. Crowchild's secret is, and I wish my thumb was half as green as hers.

I really don't need to be here. Dad agrees with me, but Mom

insists that I do. She thinks Dr. Crowchild's CBT will benefit me. CBT stands for cognitive behavioral therapy, which sounds painful, but isn't as awful as it sounds. It's supposed to help with recognizing unhealthy thought patterns and learning how to change them, but I don't see how it can help me at all. I don't have a specific fear that I need to overcome. I had a random panic attack a couple of months ago that landed me in the emergency room, and Mom freaked the heck out. All I remember from that day was feeling like I couldn't get enough air, Mom struggling to get me in the car, and then a white room where they gave me a shot of something that made my heart stop trying to run out of my chest. I was sent home with a referral to see a therapist so I could learn how to manage my anxiety and identify my triggers or whatever. Since then, I've been sitting on this couch, rubbing the frayed armrest, every second Thursday for three months now. So that's why I'm here. Mom is why I'm here.

Dr. Crowchild puts a bottle of Perrier in front of me and another on the table for herself before she sits across from me in the wingback. Her beaded chevron bracelets slide down her arm, crash into her wrist. "I'm so glad to see you again. How did you do with the homework assignment?"

I try not to roll my eyes. I've got enough real homework to do, without doing some bullshit homework for therapy sessions I don't need. Dr. Crowchild gave me a journal after my first visit with her. She said it was a thought journal, for writing down my thoughts. It sounded pretty flaky to me.

"If you write down what you're thinking, it makes you more aware of what you're thinking, which allows you to assess whether or not your thoughts are true, which is important if you're having negative thoughts."

I smiled and filed the journal in the bottom of my bag. Dad laughed when I told him. He said it sounded like a bullshit make-work project but that I should just go along with it, because Mom would be pissed at me if I didn't. So I'm going along with it.

"I couldn't think of anything to write," I say.

It's not exactly true. I didn't do it because I don't have any negative thoughts. My problem is just that I can be too sensitive. The panic attack I had that day was because I overreacted to something I shouldn't have reacted to. It's that simple. And that silly.

"That's okay," Dr. Crowchild says. "It's not always easy to find the words that define our thoughts, good or bad. It's a process."

She smiles at me, like she knows she's right, even though she isn't.

I nod. She thinks I'm agreeing with her. I'm not.

"Lexie, why don't you give it a bit more thought. Maybe next time we meet, you'll have identified a negative thought that plagues you."

I force my lips to smile. That's doubtful. I don't have any.

I can't sleep. I'm irritated that Dr. Crowchild keeps asking me to figure out what my automatic and unconscious negative thoughts are. I don't have any!

I sit up, turn on my bedside light, and dig the journal out of my bag. I flip through it; the empty pages stare back at me. Should I just make something up? Get her and Mom off my case?

Slamming it closed, I toss it on my nightstand, which knocks off the folder of Pops's puzzles, which of course lands on its end, dumping the loose paper every which way. It's super annoying, but at the same time, it reminds me that I put them there so I wouldn't forget to go through them. Clearly that didn't work. Maybe that's what I should write in my journal. That I'm forgetful. And clumsy.

Leaning over the edge of my bed, I scoop them up and spread them out on my comforter in front of me. Then I turn my phone back on and return to the website I found a couple of weeks ago and click on the submission tab.

> Please send submissions via regular mail and include a self-addressed, stamped envelope to contain your work with sufficient postage for the return of all your material. Do not send originals.

That's easy enough. I'll just pick a few of the best ones, photocopy them, and send them off. Nate doesn't need to know. That way, if nothing comes of it, he won't be disappointed.

CHAPTER ELEVEN

FRIDAY, NOVEMBER 17

The smell of butter and sugared walnuts makes my mouth water. I'm not hungry, though. Not after eating two servings of the musakhan that Zara's dad left for us before he had to run out to a meeting. Despite that, I know I'm not going to be able to resist the new recipe that Zara's mom wants me to taste test: gluten-free baklava.

"Zara and I made the phyllo pastry from scratch," her mom says. "If you like it, I'll add it to the bakery's baking list as a regular item. We need more gluten-free options on our menu."

Even though she hasn't worked at her bakery in a couple of years since her MS stole most of her independence, she still oversees the business from home and enlists Zara in helping her experiment with new recipe ideas. I watch as she makes her way to the kitchen dinette. Her hand leaves the back of the couch and grabs the counter for support before her shuffling feet follow. Zara seems unphased by the effort it takes her, but I suppose it's normal for her now. Not too long ago, she might've even been able to pass as Zara's sister, but now her curly black hair has gone dull, and wiry gray hairs have sprouted up like weeds poking through cracks in concrete. Her once well-muscled frame is long gone, as evident by the way her clothes hang on her bony hips and shoulders.

Zara places the still-warm dish on a trivet on the table, and uses a spatula to lift three pieces from the pan, depositing them on plates for each of us. Her mom slides into a chair and uses her hands to pull her uncooperative legs in the rest of the way beneath her. "In theory we should let this sit and cool off first, but I don't think we're wrong to taste test them now, don't you agree?"

"Sounds good to me," Zara says, taking the chair next to her.

I pick up the sticky treat and take a bite. The walnuts are soft and buttery and the sugar syrup oozes out, dripping down my chin. "Oh my goodness, this is so good."

"Good enough to add it to the bakery's baking list?" Zara's mom asks, one eyebrow cocked.

My head bobs up and down. "You have to make this again."

She laughs. "Done. And you're hired as my gluten-free taste tester."

After eating more baklava than we should have in one sitting, we retreat to Zara' s room. She's added a couple more photos to the clothesline that snakes across the length of the pale gray wall over her bed. I step close to study them. One is a picture of the two of us on the pool deck after practice a few weeks ago, and the other is of Zara holding a black puppy with a bright tuft of white hair on his chest.

"Is this the puppy you showed Nate and me?"

"That's him. Isn't he adorable? You're too late, though. Debbie found the perfect awesome family for him." She beams at me. "That is, unless you've changed your mind. Because I could pull some strings ..."

"No," I say. "I wish we could, but for the thousand reasons I've already told you a thousand times, we can't."

She shrugs and opens her laptop. "A new season of *The Bachelorette* starts at nine. Want to watch while we do pedicures?"

"Sure," I say.

I know better than to say no to watching Zara's favorite show. She takes these things very seriously. I enjoy watching it too, but Zara takes it to a whole other level, especially when she thinks the contestants are making the wrong choice.

"I still can't believe how the last season ended," she says. "Like, Brian? What was she thinking?" She whirls around to look at me. "And did you know they broke up a couple weeks after the show ended?" She shakes her head. "What a waste."

I giggle and flop onto her bed.

"What color do you want today? I got a couple of new ones." She rummages through the top drawer of her desk. "I'm going for Flaming Firecracker Red." She hands it to me.

"No. Not for me. Red makes me look ghoulish. Got any new pink ones?"

"A few. How about Perfect Petunia Petal Pink. Goodness. Say that ten times real fast. Or ..." She continues to rummage through her drawer. "Or these ones." She studies the stickers on the bottoms of the bottles. "Pinky Promise Pink or Pretty Piglet Pink." She rolls her eyes. "Who comes up with these names?"

I laugh.

She hands them all to me. "Here. Pick one."

She sprawls out on her fuzzy lime-green area rug beside her bed and shoves the navy throw cushion that says "Relax" in giant lime-green letters under her head. I join her on the floor and take her foot in my lap. We've done this so many times, we assume our standard positions.

I unscrew the bottle and pull the brush from the pot of dark red liquid. The distinct sweet smell of toluene fills my nostrils and I hate it and love it at the same time.

"Do you know why nail polish smells the way it does?" I ask her.

"No."

"It's the toluene. Toluene is colorless, but it's used to dissolve and suspend the pigments in the polish, and helps the polish stick to the nail. It also contributes to its glossiness once it dries."

Zara's looking at me like I just told her I was pregnant and moving to Jupiter. "Okay, Little Miss Google. Why do you know that?"

"It's about the only interesting thing I've learned so far in chemistry."

"Why'd you take that again?"

"I don't know."

I'm careful to wipe the excess from the brush before I place it at the base of her nail and drag it up toward me. She shoves her door closed with her other foot.

"All right. We're alone now, so talk. I want all the juicy details."

A snort laugh escapes my throat. I can't help teasing her. "I'm not sure what the other chemicals are. I'd have to look them up."

It's a good thing the bottle in my hand isn't a real firecracker, because the way she jerks her foot back and props herself up on her elbows would've set it off. The space between her eyebrows is missing as she whisper-yells at me. "You know exactly who and which juicy details I'm talking about."

She's not wrong to assume there are details. Since our kiss on the path, I've met Rhys at the pool twice more, and both times we ended up kissing. The last time, just two days ago, we ended up at the playground, me pressed between him and the giant orange plastic tube slide, and his hands went on an exploratory search under my sweater.

On the nights I haven't seen him, and haven't been busy helping Dad, I've stayed up late into the night texting with him, trading details with each other like how I used to trade stickers and Shopkins with girls on the playground. I told him that I hate avocados but like guacamole, and he told me that he has dyseidetic dyslexia. I told him I've been carrying a sketchbook around since I was four, and he told me he's allergic to kiwis. I told him that when I was little, my favorite thing to draw was my family but I'd often forget to draw their arms. He laughed and told me that before he played guitar, he played the bagpipes.

I grab her ankle, pulling her foot back in my lap. "Will you relax? You're going to get red polish everywhere."

A furious look dances in her eyes, but she obliges.

"Talk," she says, lying back down on her pillow. "Tell. Me. Everything."

I hesitate, try to decide how much to tell her.

"There isn't much to tell."

Lie.

"We've met at the pool a couple more times, but that's about it."

Lie.

It's not that I want to keep it secret from her, I just don't want her to worry that things are moving too fast, because I know that's what she'll think, and to be honest, even though she has a right to know as my BFF, I'd rather keep some things for just me, otherwise it's less special somehow.

"So, nothing more has happened since your first kiss? He hasn't tried to put his hands into places they shouldn't go?"

My breath stalls. She's stated the truth, and I focus harder on her toes.

"No."

Lie.

I blow on her toes and inspect my polish job. "Give me your other foot." I gesture with my hand to get her to switch feet.

"That's a relief," she says. "I've heard rumors that he's a bit of a player."

"Who told you that?"

"A few people. People who know people from his other school. Kara said he dated a bunch of girls. That he wasn't the type of guy to stick with just one. That he's the kind of guy that has a girl but never has a girlfriend."

"He's not like that, Zara."

She tilts her head, a silent challenge to what I know.

"He isn't. At least not with me."

I place her now-polished second foot flat on the floor and fan her toes with the folding fan we keep for this purpose.

"As long as you're sure."

"I am. Don't worry." I tap her feet. "You're done."

She hands me the pillow and I hand her the bottle of Perfect Petunia Pink. Cold polish spreads out across the nail bed of my big toe. She changes the subject.

"Did you submit your application?"

Anxiety punches me and a shard of irritation jabs me, that she's asking about this again. Applications are due at the end of the month. I'm running out of time to tell Dad what I need to tell him. At least I got my sketches and paintings for my portfolio done.

"Yup."

Another lie. It's getting so much easier.

Relief washes over her face. "I've been meaning to ask you how it went. You know, with your dad."

"It went fine. Like you said. I was worried for nothing."

Lie. Lie. Lie. Lies. They're coming out so easily now, just sliding off my tongue, like secrets whispered in the dark.

She swats my ankle. "You see? And you were so worried."

She says it in a way that says, do you see now, you're crazy?

I force a laugh and she blows on my toes. I think she's probably right, and hope that one day I'll believe her for real.

CHAPTER TWELVE

SATURDAY, NOVEMBER 25

When Dad announces he has a surprise for me and Jonah, I'm even more surprised that it involves wearing blindfolds and being driven to a mystery location. But when we get out of the car and are guided inside a building, I immediately know where we are. The sound of a dog barking is a dead giveaway, but even without that, the competing scents of antiseptic, kibble, and wet dog tell me everything I need to know. I'm on high alert, trying to arrange the pieces of this puzzle together, but I can't get them to fit. The reality crystallizes for me, though, when Dad instructs us to take off our blindfolds and Debbie and Zara are standing in front of us. Zara's holding the black puppy with the tuft of white chest hair, her face exploding with a smile as big as the sun.

"Surprise!" she squeals, vibrating almost as much as the puppy. She rushes at me, pressing her lips to my ear, the puppy squished between us. He licks my chin. "You're the perfect family I told you about!"

Wait. What?

I pull away and search her face, trying to take stock of this impossible scenario. Jonah's eyes are flicking back and forth between us and Dad. "He's ours?"

"Yes. He's yours!" Zara squeals, transferring the squirming ball of black fluff into Jonah's arms.

My eyes snap to Dad. He's watching me, a grin plastered wide on his face.

"Happy birthday, Lexie. I know it's not for another month, but Maverick couldn't wait, and I know how much you've been wanting a dog."

My mind's still trying to catch up on what I'm missing. I've wanted a dog? He must be confused. It's Jonah who has always wanted a dog.

Jonah's now laying flat on the floor, giggling while Maverick dances and wiggles all around and over him, licking his face whenever he lunges in close.

"What's wrong, Lexie?" Dad's eyes have gone dark, his voice rough. "You don't want him?"

His accusation crashes like a pile of rocks at my feet and everybody's gaze swivels to land on me. Even Maverick stops and stares at me, but it's Dad's gaze that burns the hottest. My stomach flips inside out. He doesn't need to say anything. I know what he wants, what's expected of me.

"Sorry, Jonah," Dad says, his pointed stare glued on me, "but the deal's off if Lexie's not on board. He's her birthday present, after all."

Fury rolls off Jonah in waves. If he had hackles, they'd be on end. "What the hell, Lexie! Why don't you want him?"

Bile foams in my gut and my thoughts tumble every which way as I try to work out how I'm going to fit a dog into my already too-jam-packed life. I want to tell him all the reasons why we can't take him. Why I can't take him. That next year I'll be even busier and have even less time to give to a dog. But I know I can't tell him that; I know better than to decline a gift from Dad. The much bigger issue, though, is Jonah. He'll never forgive me if I don't agree, and I can't live with that. I know I have a choice, but I don't think I do.

I brave his gaze and pinch my lips up into a smile. He won't know it's fake. He never looks at the quality of my reactions, just that I provide the right one.

"Of course I want him," I lie. "Why wouldn't I?"

Instantly the vice pressing in on all sides of the room releases, the gray clouds disperse and the sun comes back. Jonah's face cracks in half with a grin that just about swallows his face.

"Yes! We can keep you, buddy!" He throws himself at Maverick, wrapping his arms around his neck. Dad's stare slides away from me.

There. I did it. I said the right thing. The foaming sea sloshing in my gut subsides. Just remember to be the Lexie he wants me to be and everything will be fine.

I crouch down on the floor next to Jonah, and Maverick bounces to me, puts his paws on my shoulders, and slurps my face. I fall backward and he flops over, landing in my lap, legs in the air, belly exposed for rubbing.

Debbie laughs and claps her hands together. "I can already see that he's going to fit in so well with you."

Zara says something too, but I don't hear her because I'm too busy wondering how Debbie seems to not be at all concerned about the fake life Dad told her we have.

Gran and Uncle John arrive soon after we get home. Turns out Dad arranged for them to come with a cake for me to mark my birthday properly, even though I don't turn sixteen until after Christmas. The voice in my head that's Dad's reminds me that it's fine, that it doesn't matter when we celebrate it, that it's the thought that counts.

While Jonah tries to convince Maverick to pee, I go inside and sit with Gran. She hands me a bright red envelope.

"It's from your Uncle John and me. We didn't know what to get you, so we gave you money so you can get whatever you want."

I tell her thanks and lean over to give her a hug.

"What are you going to spend it on? Some new earphone things, or maybe something for your swimming? I keep asking your dad to bring me to one of your swimming events, but it never seems to work out."

"That would be great," I say.

I don't bother telling her that I've also been waiting for Dad to come to one of my events.

"I'm training for a big meet in the spring. You should come to that one. There's even a couple of scholarships available. Coach says I have a pretty good chance."

Gran's eyes light up. "A scholarship? To what, dear?"

Dad puts a steaming mug on the table in front of Gran. Uncle John stands next to him, a beer in his hand. "Scholarship for what?" he asks.

His question lands with a thud at my feet and everything I've been wanting to tell him scrambles into a pile in my head. I work to organize it all quickly, properly, so the words that need to be said come out the right way, so there's no way he can misunderstand. It helps that Gran's here, because telling him through her is going to make it easier.

I do my best to ignore Dad's stabbing eyes and focus on Gran. I repeat what I told Dad last spring, and then again after Mom and I went to the info night that he couldn't, or rather wouldn't, come to.

"And the best part is that it'll allow me to earn a credit or two toward my BA before I even finish high school."

Gran's eyes are wide, her smile infringing on her ears. Dad, though, is looking at me like I'm speaking gibberish and I want to kick myself that once again I didn't explain it well enough to sell him on the idea.

"But it's far away, and there's no bus from here," he says, ignoring all the good things I said.

I press my lips closed, holding back details that I know won't help my case. The reality is that it's not far at all. Not from Mom's house.

"And what happens if you don't get a scholarship?" he asks. "Who will pay for it?"

Gran's smile slips off her face and she seems to shrink into the cushions.

He continues, his face smeared with smug. "It doesn't make sense that you go there when you can finish high school here. For free."

No. No, no, no. I need to clarify, make him understand. I balance my words just right, like how I used to balance Jenga blocks with Jonah.

"I could, but —" My words tumble out, crash into a pile.

He waves his hand, like he's shooing an annoying fly. "All the schools teach the same thing. They just say they're different to justify people paying for something they can have for free. And," he says, a smile creeping up one side of his face, "do you need a fancy art school? I've taught you everything you need to know about how to paint. Going to some overpriced school to learn how to draw and paint pictures in those books you carry around isn't going to get you anywhere."

His face screws up, like he thinks it's silly. "Not to mention that I need you here to help with the business like you promised. At least until I can hire more people. You understand that, don't you?"

Gran's nodding now, accepting Dad's reasoning. Guilt rises in me hard and fast and I feel my head bobbing up and down reflexively, trying to diffuse a situation that's going downhill fast.

"Your dad has a point, dear," Gran says. "It would be easier for him if you just stayed at the school here."

I tell myself they're not wrong, but I can't help wanting what I want for me. Of course, I understand that he needs my help, even though I don't remember promising to help the way he seems to think I did. I don't say anything more, though, because guilt at my selfishness moves in, trapping the words I want to say in a ball of shame that gets stuck in my throat.

It's after Gran and Uncle John leave that I have a stroke of brilliance. I realize that I don't have to tell him that I'm applying because applying doesn't equal acceptance. Why rock a boat that might not even set sail? Breath comes back into my body, the stress of it all lifted.

I'll tell him *if* I get accepted, which I won't know until March. By then he'll have hired more people and won't need my help like he does now. In the meantime, I'll devote all my extra free time to help him launch his business, just like he says I promised I would. That way, when he sees how supportive and helpful I am, helping him get what he wants, he won't be able to say no to me. It's only fair. If I play my cards right, this should all work out just fine.

CHAPTER THIRTEEN

DECEMBER TO JANUARY

The weeks go by in a blur. November seeps into December and people replace their gourds and pumpkins with Santa hats and snowmen. I turn sixteen on my actual birthday, and Mom gets me the new swimsuit and the brown calf-high boots I wanted. Nate and his dad get approval for the loan they need to renovate the OldMill, and we, or rather Nate and Zara, solidify plans to host the regatta to coincide with the grand opening on Canada Day weekend. When Jonah hears that the regatta is a go, he drags Mom to the hardware store to get sheets of cardboard, rolls of duct tape, and paint, and takes over the basement, finishing the cardboard rendition of his dirt bike, complete with sidecar, in a matter of days.

The new year comes and goes and I swap out chem for world history, thank goodness, but I hardly notice because I'm so exhausted from helping Dad and trying to housebreak a puppy at the same time. All the puppy books say to take your puppy out every hour when housebreaking. What they don't tell you is that most of the time, the puppy will get distracted by every snowflake that blows by and wait till after you go back inside to do his business on the floor. It's okay, though. I'm managing. I'm even finding time to sneak away to see Rhys. The important thing is that everybody has what they need from me, so everybody's happy. Everyone, that is, except Mom.

"I don't like this," Mom says, making tiny circles in the air with her index finger when I decline her offer of a ride to practice again.

"What's 'this'?" I copy her finger motion, feigning ignorance, even though I know what she's talking about. I know she hates that.

"You missing practice. It's not like you. And you haven't been to the marina in weeks."

It's not the first time she's mentioned my busyness. She's starting to get all nosy and controlling like she always does. Dad predicted she would, and once again, he was right. It's why he didn't want us to tell her about Mav, but I told him we had to. It was the only way to get her to let us spend the extra time we needed to at his house.

"You're making a big deal out of nothing again. I promise I'll get to the next practice."

I say this knowing it's likely a promise I won't be able to keep, but I need to get her off my back. She looks at me, her eyes probing into my head. I hate when she does that. I always wonder if she might see something I don't want her to see. She seems to have a way of knowing things about me that I don't even know.

"I'm holding you to that, Lexie," she says.

Zara mentions it too, during one of our FT conversations.

"Coach is noticing. You can't miss more than two practices and expect that he won't."

Knots coil in my stomach. I'd missed a few dates with Mr. Harris too. Too many. Dad promised he'd get me to practice last week, but then an order of drywall was being delivered and he had to be there to sign for it.

"Sorry, Lexie," he said. "It's not a big deal though, right? Aren't you already the best swimmer on the team? Do you even need to go?"

I nodded and told him it was fine, even though it wasn't. I didn't want to be a bother.

"Things are super busy right now, Lexie, and this is a team effort." His eyes went soft. "I couldn't have gotten this far without you. You know that, right?"

A warm feeling spread through me when he said that, because it proved he saw my efforts. I just need to keep it up a bit longer, balance all the things, to show him that I can manage a busy schedule; that if he needs me, I can do both. I need him to understand that me going to Sunridge isn't going to change who he needs me to be.

CHAPTER FOURTEEN

THURSDAY, FEBRUARY 1

The day started crappy and got a whole lot worse. My alarm didn't go off, and since I'm the only one in the house with an alarm clock, we were all late. It seems that alarm clocks stop working when your dog chews the wires while you're busy trying to get your English assignment done. I scrambled out of bed, but tripped pulling on my favorite leggings, ripping them in the process. And if that wasn't bad enough, Mav pooped right in front of my door. There was no way to open it without spreading the problem over a greater area, if you know what I mean. Needless to say, I was late for first period world history.

I'm just about out the door at lunch to go home to let Mav out when I get called over the school intercom to report to the guidance office.

"Lexie, thanks for coming. Have a seat." Ms. Emerson gestures to a chair facing her desk. I perch on the chair and give her a tight smile. I hope she can tell that I need her to make this quick. She laces her fingers together and leans forward.

"How are you, Lexie?"

"I'm fine. I was late this morning because my dog —"

"It's not about this morning. I just wanted to check in with you. Make sure everything's okay." Her voice goes up a bit at the end, like it's a question. I stare at her blankly. She changes course.

"Is your hope still to go to Sunridge?"

My stomach pulls and my armpits get damp. "Yes. Why wouldn't it be?"

"Sunridge is asking for copies of updated transcripts by the end of February," she says, sliding a piece of paper across her desk to me. "You must know that your grades have slipped since you applied in November, and —"

I stop listening and snatch the paper from her desk. Have they? I know I've been a bit distracted, but for the most part I've been getting my work done.

"All of your teachers have said that you seem distracted, and you haven't been to lunchtime study hall in weeks."

Her voice sounds far away, like she's in a cave, and a wave of dizziness comes over me.

"Lexie, this has serious implications on your plans for next year. If you don't get your grades back up, it's possible that it will affect Sunridge's decision."

I tune her out, close my eyes, take deep breaths. I'm back in Dr. Crowchild's office and we're practicing the deep breathing technique.

"Remember, when you feel like things are spiraling out of control, breathe in, hold for five seconds, and then out."

"Lexie? Lexie, are you okay? Let me get you some water."

When my head stops spinning and my heart stops crashing around, I open my eyes. A bottle of water appears in front of me. I take it and gulp down half of it.

Ms. Emerson's perched on the corner of her desk beside me, her face creased with worry.

"Thanks. I haven't eaten yet today. I feel a little woozy."

"Oh goodness, here," she says, reaching behind her to open the top drawer of her desk. She hands me an apple. "I didn't intend to take you from your lunch break."

I bite into it greedily.

"It's not too late to turn this around, Lexie."

"I'll fix it. I promise. I've just been so busy that I didn't realize …"

She smiles. "It's okay. I figured you'd gotten a little sidetracked. You can't fix a problem if you're not aware there's a problem, right? I need you to talk to all your teachers and find out what you need to do to get back on track."

I nod.

"I haven't told your parents, but I will if I don't see improvement in the next couple of weeks. Maybe you could start by getting back to lunchtime study hall. It'll send a strong message to your teachers that you're serious."

I nod, not because I agree with her, but because she expects me to. I can't go to lunchtime study hall. If I don't go home to let Mav out for a pee and to restuff his Kong with something delicious like peanut butter or cut-up hot dogs, then there's going to be an even bigger mess for me to deal with at the end of the day.

"I'll do my best," I say.

"I'm glad to hear that. Please come see me if I can help in any way."

Before the school day is over, I talk to all my teachers. Each of them gives me either the opportunity to redo an assignment, or something entirely new to do. While I'm grateful they're giving me the chance to catch back up, the pressure is even greater since everything is due in three short weeks.

CHAPTER FIFTEEN

MONDAY, FEBRUARY 5

Mom's waiting for me outside the school's main doors after last period.

"Get in." She leans over to push the passenger door open from the driver's seat.

"Why are you here?" I bend down to look at her through the open door.

"Your English teacher called me."

Crap.

"Then I called your other teachers. Enough's enough. First it's swim practice, now this? Get in."

"I've got it under control, Mom."

"I hope you're right. But in the meantime, Dr. Crowchild agreed to see you. I'm taking you to her now."

I roll my eyes, not caring that she sees. I don't have time for an appointment with a therapist I don't need, but the look on her face tells me I've lost. I get in and yank the car door shut. If she wants to control my life, I'm not going to make it easy for her, or be happy about it.

Dr. Crowchild puts a bottle of Perrier in front of me and another on the table for herself before she sits across from me in her usual chair, with the same notebook and pen balanced on her lap. I'm sitting in my usual place, fiddling with the loose string on the armrest, a throw cushion decorated with orange, blue, and yellow beads stitched in a pattern of repeated circles in my lap.

"It's nice to see you again, Lexie. How have you been?"

I shrug. "Fine."

"I'm happy to hear that. How's your anxiety been? Have you needed to make use of any of the strategies we practiced?"

"It's been okay."

She nods and jots something down on her notepad.

"How's school? Did you do okay on your Chem final? I know Chemistry was tough."

My eyes snap up from the loose thread I'm fiddling with to meet hers. "How do you know about that? Did my mom tell you something about my grades?"

She startles at my reaction. "No. I'm asking about chemistry because you mentioned it was your worst subject. I told you that calculus was mine. Remember?"

Relief washes over me that Mom didn't overstep, but now I feel stupid, because I've just given her dirt on me that I didn't want her to have.

"Oh, right. I forgot about that."

She smiles and takes a sip of her water. I do the same.

"That's all right. If I didn't write things down," she taps her notepad with her pen, "I wouldn't remember things either.

Which reminds me, have you found writing in your journal helpful? Were you able to identify any of your automatic negative thoughts?" She flips through her notebook. "I have written here that you hadn't used the journal yet, and you'd give some more thought as to what some of your automatic negative thoughts might be."

No. You said I should do that. I didn't say that.

"I haven't had a chance yet," I say. "I've been busy."

Because how is writing about the anxiety I feel about not getting my assignments done on time going to help me get them done on time?

"I was hoping to spend tonight getting some of my homework done, but my mom decided my time was better spent here."

I can't keep my annoyance from leaking out. I direct my eyes away from her, stare at the network of spider cracks that creep along her ceiling.

Dr. Crowchild scribbles more stuff on her notepad about me.

"So, you don't think being here with me right now is a good use of your time?"

Her eyes search my face, like she's looking for inventory, and I can't help feeling guilty about wanting to do something other than sit here. The truth is that I do want to please her and tell her that my anxiety hasn't been great. That it feels like my butterflies are always on call, but that I'm managing. It's Mom who refuses to believe it. Maybe she should be the one sitting in here. I push my sleeves up and take another sip of water. All of a sudden it's too warm in here. Like, jeez. Dad's right. Mom's always looking for problems where there aren't any. I wish she'd just butt out and leave me alone. I put my water bottle back on the table in front of me.

"That's right. I don't mean to sound ungrateful, but I've got lots of homework I should be working on right now."

And I need to finish painting the doorjambs, start my makeup assignments, and find time to take Mav to the park.

"I see. Thank you for being honest with me. I appreciate that you have a heavy course load and I won't keep you much longer."

She shifts in her chair, making the tassels on her beaded tan suede moccasins bounce.

"May I ask what's got you so busy that you've fallen behind on your schoolwork?"

I pull out my phone and show her a picture of Mav. Her face lights up.

"It's no wonder you're so busy! What's his or her name?"

She reaches behind her for her own cellphone.

"Maverick. But I call him Mav."

She turns her phone to me.

"These are my two. Jack and Jill. They're not puppies anymore, but they were a big handful when they were." She shakes her head like she's glad that time is over and puts her phone back. "Dogs are wonderful, but they require a lot of our time. Could it be that the puppy's taking too much of your time?"

My back teeth grind together. If she wasn't sitting in front of me, I'd swear Mom had taken her place.

"No. It's not just Maverick that's keeping me busy. There are other things too."

"Oh. Like what?" She leans forward in her chair, her chin on her fist.

I hesitate, not sure that I want to tell her more than I already have. That it's safe to tell her Dad's secrets.

"It's up to you what you choose to share, or not share, with me," she says, like she can read my mind. "But I will remind you what I told you when I saw you the first time. Everything you tell me stays in here. Confidential. That is unless I have reason to believe you are at risk of harming yourself or others, or if I believe you are at risk in some way. In those cases, I'm bound by my licensing body, and I have a duty to report."

There's something about the way she looks at me, the softness in her eyes, that makes me believe she genuinely wants to help me.

"So, you won't tell my parents what we talk about? Even though my mom's paying for this?"

"That's right. What you tell me stays between us."

I nod, consider what she's saying.

"And what happens if you do?"

"I could lose my license."

I feel safer hearing that and decide that I do want to vent to her. That maybe her advice could be useful.

"It's nothing bad. I'm just super busy right now helping my dad. He started his own renovation business and he needed my brother and me to help get it started. We've been helping him after school and on weekends. It's why I'm so busy. I can't tell my mom, because she and my dad don't get along, and if she knows, it'll complicate things."

Her head bobs up and down vigorously. "Thank you for trusting me with that. That's very good of you that you're willing to help your dad as much as you are. Most girls your age wouldn't be so willing, but I'll bet he's teaching you all kinds of valuable life skills."

Words escape me for a moment and I just stare at her. I can't believe she just said that. She's just validated what my life's been like for the past few months. Sure, I'm busy helping him, but I'm getting benefit from it too. It's this moment that makes me realize that she'll understand what Mom never will, and maybe Mom was right, forcing me to come here. Maybe Dr. Crowchild can give me some strategies to help me talk to Dad better.

"Yeah. He told me that he wouldn't be where he is right now if it wasn't for me and all the work I've done."

I smile inside, remembering.

A smile pushes her cheeks up. "It's wonderful that you and your dad have such a good relationship and that you can help him like that. It does feel wonderful when we're acknowledged for the efforts we put in, doesn't it?"

I shrug like it's not a big deal, even though it's everything.

"Is it possible though, that the time spent helping your dad is taking too much time away from your own priorities? It seems like what you're telling me is that your dad's priorities have become your priorities."

She tilts her head, studying me, like she didn't just drop a lit explosive on the table between us. I deny it in my head. I tell myself that what she said is ridiculous, that my priorities haven't changed, but expanded. That I want him to want me, but I wish he needed a little less of me.

I shake my head. "No. My priorities are still the same. I just need to manage my time better."

"I see. Would you say that you've taken on too many things?"

Have I? No. He needs me.

I look at my lap. "I guess. Maybe."

"Have you told your dad that?"

That's not something I can tell him.

"Not like that, no."

She says nothing. She just stares at me, like she's waiting for me to finish.

"How do I tell him that? He's on so many deadlines."

"And you're not on deadlines?"

I blink at her. She says it like she thinks my deadlines are somehow just as important as his. The room tilts as my brain tries to piece together the preposterous idea she's proposing.

"Have you said, 'Dad, I have to get my homework done first, and if I have time after that, I'll help you'?"

"Don't be selfish, Lexie. The business, which is going to pay for our rent and groceries, is obviously more important than your swim, or your little essay. Get your priorities straight."

I look at her, and my eyebrows squish together.

"No. Not exactly."

"Why not?"

"I don't know. He needs me. I don't want to disappoint him."

Her eyebrows raise up a notch. "So are you saying that you feel like you don't have a choice?"

"No. It's not that. I just don't want to be selfish. If people know I'm busy but still ask for my help, it must mean it's super important. They wouldn't ask otherwise."

Her forehead creases. "So, you believe it's selfish to say no when someone asks something of you?"

"Isn't it?"

She gets up from her chair to grab a book from the shelf behind her desk.

"I'm going to read to you the definition of selfish from the dictionary." She sits back down across from me and flips through the pages. "'A selfish person is primarily interested in them-self: Someone concentrating on their own advantage without considering others.'" She looks up at me. "Does that sound like you, Lexie? Based on what you've told me, it seems like you have so much consideration for your dad's priorities that it's at the expense of yourself."

Wait. What?

A sliver of doubt wriggles around in my brain, cramming itself next to my wedge of loyalty.

She studies me, her eyes filled with genuine concern. "Our time's up now, but I hope you come back next week. I'd like to talk about this some more. In the meantime, I want you to try to put yourself and your priorities ahead of the needs of other people. You're allowed to set your own goals for your future self. It isn't selfish to do that."

She pauses, holds the door open for me.

"And consider this possibility: Is believing you're selfish one of your automatic negative thoughts?"

CHAPTER SIXTEEN

TUESDAY, FEBRUARY 13

His back is to me when I pause at his open door. Even though it's only been a month since I saw him last, he looks different. Older. Somehow smaller. Like his wheelchair's swallowing him. And despite the warmth of his room, the threadbare plaid blanket that's normally folded and draped over the end of his bed is tucked around his legs, his slippered feet sticking out beneath it.

He's not ready for me like he usually is, which makes me feel even guiltier. I want to kick myself for letting him down. I didn't intend to miss so many of our Scrabble dates, but there was always something that I was needed for. The first two times it was Dad that needed me: once to help him hang cabinets, the other to help him buy some tools. It's a good thing I went with him, though, because he would've paid double the price for the name-brand tools, rather than the knockoff versions I found for him for half the price. The third time was because Nate, Zara, and I hadn't been able to touch base about our regatta planning in forever (my fault). And last week I was on my way here after school when Rhys surprised me, pulling up in front of me at the bus stop, inviting me out for frozen yogurt. The look on the faces of the two grade twelve girls who were waiting with me — both of them with perfect hair and makeup, wearing their Lulu tights with their bright Converse sneakers in the melting snow — was priceless. He leaned over to talk to me through his passenger window.

"Hey, gorgeous. Can I take you for some Froyo?"

"I can't today, remember?" I said, resting my forearms on the door. "I told you, I have my thing at the nursing home."

His lips pinched up. "Right. I forgot that's a thing you do."

I nodded.

"I'm sure they won't mind if you miss a week. Besides, I have band commitments the rest of the week, so today's the only day I can see you."

I didn't want to miss another visit with Mr. Harris, but at the same time, I didn't want to give Rhys the impression that I didn't want to see him. He obviously forgot that I had a commitment.

"Are you going to make me beg? Don't you want to see me today?"

"Of course I do," I said, shoving my guilt about Mr. Harris aside and climbing in the car beside him.

I'd been doing that a lot lately, shoving guilt into a little box inside my head. It was becoming full. Almost too full to close. But what could I do? I didn't have much choice at the moment. If I refused, he'd have thought that he wasn't a priority for me, and what kind of girlfriend would do that? So I went with him, and after we finished at Froyo's, he took me to our spot under the giant willow tree that overlooks the lake. It's tucked away at the end of a tiny long-ago-closed road that follows the curve of the south side of the lake. Its long, wispy branches swayed in the breeze and brushed against the car, like a curtain, shrouding us in privacy. There, he reminded me how much he missed me and let me prove to him that he's a big priority in my life.

So today is Tuesday. Again. This morning, I promised myself that no matter what or who happened, I was going to see Mr. Harris. Nobody and nothing was going to stop me.

I tap at his door, and keep tapping, louder and louder, until he turns.

"Huh. Look who decided to show up."

I smile and my butterflies get ready to initiate their symphony.

"I'm surprised to see you at all, given you stood me up the last four weeks."

"I'm sorry."

That's the truth.

"It couldn't be helped. I've been super busy."

Also the truth.

"I've been in the pool almost every day —"

A blatant lie.

"— and —"

"I had to play Scrabble with that other kid, Jamieson, whatever. What a waste of time that was. He'd never played before, if that tells you how well that went."

He gestures with his hands as he often does when he gets excited or annoyed. With him it's hard to tell which it is sometimes. The tubing running from the oxygen tank behind him to his nose jostles around and he readjusts it, setting it back in its proper place.

"I'm here if you want to play now."

It's not a question, but it comes out like one.

He stares at me hard. I look at my shoes.

"Harmph." He turns the wheels of his chair toward the small table in the corner of his room. I adjust my backpack and lean on the doorframe, uncertain of what I should do.

"Are you going to stand there, or are you going to come in and play with me?"

The invitation to play tells me I'm forgiven. My butterflies take their seats, their symphony forgotten.

"Grab the board from the shelf. I had the support worker put it away after you didn't show up the second time. I couldn't stomach another game with that kid. I eventually took mercy on him and suggested we play chess instead, but he didn't know how to do that either! Can you believe that?"

He throws me a scowl, but I see his usual sarcastic playfulness dance in his eyes, so I know his gruffness is just his usual, and not directed at me specifically.

I put the game on the table for him and he starts setting it up. I busy myself tidying his room and watering his plant while I wait.

"For goodness sake. It doesn't need water. Can't you see that it's dead?"

I roll my eyes. Here we go again. I think the only reason he agreed to keep the plant is because he enjoys arguing about it with me.

"No, it isn't. I know there are some flowers in there. I just need to find them."

He clicks his tongue. "When are you going to understand that you can't make something out of nothing? You need to learn to stop watering dead things."

CHAPTER SEVENTEEN

FRIDAY, FEBRUARY 16

"He'd better not give her a rose. She's such a snob. Can you believe what she did to Tanya last week?"

I'm only half paying attention to Zara as she examines herself in the mirror while we watch an episode of *The Bachelor* and plan out what we (mostly she) plans to wear to what she keeps telling me is the most important social event of the year, happening in two weeks. I'd asked her why we couldn't just figure out our wardrobe the day of the party, and she looked at me like she'd never heard anything so ridiculous.

"If we wait till then to find out that our closets are lacking something essential, it'll be too late to do anything about it, and that would be dumb."

I didn't argue with her. What was the point?

"You have to come, Lexie," she says. "It's mostly a Sunridge crowd, so we can get ahead on the social scene if you come with me. I can introduce you to all the VIPs."

Zara throws a wine-colored sweater at me. "Try that on. It'll be perfect with your leggings and those brown boots your mom got you for your birthday."

She studies me as I put it on. "What's up with you lately?"

"What do you mean?"

"You're here, but not here. Nate and I hardly see you anymore. And you've missed a lot of swim."

I bristle. She sounds a little too much like Mom.

"His name is Maverick. Remember him? I'm pretty sure it was you that had a hand in creating the preoccupation you claim I'm stuck in." I can't help the snark that comes out.

"I get it. But what I don't get is how getting a puppy means the rest of your life stops."

Her words are like a splash of cold water, and I hear Dr. Crowchild's voice in my head.

"Are you sure you haven't replaced your priorities with your dad's priorities?"

I assure myself again that she got it wrong, but it takes me longer to convince myself.

"I'm worried about you, Lexie. That's all."

Craning her head around, she looks over her shoulder at the full-length mirror that hangs on the back of her bedroom door. "Do these pants squash my butt too much?"

I laugh. "No. They've got enough stretch that they're hugging you in all the right places. You have to make those your new best-butt pants."

She nods and runs a hand over her butt like she's smoothing away an imaginary wrinkle. Satisfied, she turns back around. "I'll wear these. What do you think of that sweater I tossed you?" She opens one of her dresser drawers and pulls out a pair of black leggings that glitter subtly when the light hits them the right way. "Try these with it."

I oblige her, because I won't hear the end of it if I don't. Standing in front of her mirror, I'm pleasantly surprised. The sweater is a lower cut than I usually wear, but not so much that it looks like the shirt's purpose is to show off my boobs. It's perfectly revealing, if that's a thing. Like Zara's jeans, it clings to me in all the right places and is long enough that it covers most of my butt, and it goes fantastic with her leggings. She's not wrong about the boots Mom got me. They'll finish off the outfit perfectly.

Zara lets out a squeal of delight. "Oh, that's perfect on you. Now just …" She reaches up and pulls the elastic holding my ponytail out. Using her fingers, she tousles my hair. "There. Now that's perfect."

Taking the elastic from her, I secure it in its place around my wrist. She's convinced me about the clothes. The hair thing, not so much.

CHAPTER EIGHTEEN

FRIDAY, FEBRUARY 23

I'm so focused on my homework that I don't notice Dad and Jonah have made it home until Dad's standing beside my desk and Mav's tail is thumping everything within a three-foot radius. I feel the regular pull in my stomach. He never comes into my room unless he needs something.

I pull out my earbuds, force a smile. "What's up?"

He can't contain the grin that swallows his face. "I've got good news. Come downstairs. Family meeting."

I look at my binder. I'm almost done. Just three more problems. In another twenty minutes I'll be in a good spot to take a quick break before I tackle the last extra assignment I need to get done by Monday: write an essay discussing the main themes in the short story "The Yellow Wallpaper."

"It's not selfish to put your priorities first, Lexie."

"Can you give me twenty minutes?" I ask.

His gaze stiffens on mine and his lips fold shut. My gut kicks my stomach. I think fast, double back.

"Never mind. This can wait."

I get up to follow him downstairs and his face goes back to normal, my mistake erased. My stomach unwinds.

Downstairs, Jonah's waiting for us on the couch. I perch on the duct-taped arm of the chair next to him. Dad's too worked up to sit. He clasps his hands together in front of him.

"I've picked up a big job. One that's going to put our business on the map."

"What is it?" Jonah's knees bounce up and down.

"But we're growing so fast that I need to hire someone to help run the business side of things," Dad says. "I need a website and business cards, and someone to respond to potential clients and ..."

I'm half listening, my mind busy working out which themes I should focus on for my essay.

"What do you think?"

He's looking at me. Instantly I'm on high alert, and I scramble to catch up.

"About what?"

He tilts his head to his shoulder, annoyed. "About you managing the business side of things until I can hire someone."

A brick drops through my stomach.

Oh no. No no no no no.

"It'll be easy for you. You've been working at that marina for years now. It's a no-brainer that you be the one to do it."

"It isn't selfish to say no, Lexie."

My already sloshy stomach turns into a churning whirlpool. My butterflies, their wings sodden, flap clumsily about.

I can't agree to this. I have to do what's best for me. I have to tell him. I wipe my wet palms on my pants, take a deep breath, and try to drum up confidence I don't have.

"I can't. I'm too busy right now. I wish I could" — *Lie. No, I don't* — "but I can't. I'm sorry."

Lie. I'm not sorry. I'm glad your business is working out, even though I wish it would just fall apart.

He studies me, his eyes small slits, and I lean farther back on the chair's arm, increasing the distance between us. I brace myself for the rage that I know is coming. Except it doesn't come. Instead, his eyes soften and guilt shines in them.

"I'm sorry, Lexie. I know I'm asking a lot, but there's no one else that can do it. I need you now, more than ever. Please don't let me down. It'll just be for a little while, until I find someone else to take the job." His eyes plead with mine. "I'm only able to do this now because of you, and all the work you've already done."

"Well, me too, right, Dad?" says Jonah.

Dad doesn't even look at my brother.

"Don't kid yourself, Lexie. You're so smart. If anyone can do it, it's you."

I bend like a tree in a hurricane. His approval is all it takes for my mouth to disconnect from my brain, which is screaming at me to say, "No Dad, I can't take on more stuff for you because you're killing my ability to be me," and I feel myself nodding, like it's a reflex. I can't let him down now. He needs me. What kind of person would I be if I said no?

"I guess I could find a couple hours to —"

"Great!" Dad says, his face splitting with a smile. "I knew I could count on you."

The smile on his face, which I put there, is worth all the sleepless nights, the missed swim practices and extra assignments. I can pretend I'm fine with it for a little bit longer, and then I'll be free. The twisty whirlpool in my gut settles. I tell myself that everything will be fine and I think I even believe it.

CHAPTER NINETEEN

SATURDAY, FEBRUARY 24

"Lexie!"

I jolt awake. Sunlight assaults my eyes and I blink to clear them.

"Why are you still in bed?" Dad asks. "I thought it was clear last night that I needed your help today."

A quick look at my phone tells me it's nine thirty. I push myself up. At least I got a couple hours of sleep. I rub my eyes. "What do you need?"

"The license and insurance stuff. I can't start this new job until I submit those documents."

I nod, but I can't remember him telling me anything about a license or insurance, or any documents for that matter. Did I zone out of that part of yesterday's conversation? I don't want him to think I wasn't paying attention.

"I'm on it." I scootch my way around Mav, who's still lying on his back, front legs pointed to the ceiling. "Should I just scan and email them?"

"Sure, but after you create them, let me see them before you scan them."

Wait. What?

Time slows while I try to sort out why I'm confused. It's like I've been given a puzzle that's missing a bunch of pieces.

"What do you mean, create them?" I ask.

He huffs out a sigh. "Lexie, we talked about this. I don't have a contractor's license or insurance. I need you to make it look like I do, so the new owner of the OldMill will hire me. He's already said the job's mine. The paperwork's just a formality."

My lungs clench and my heart stalls. Sweat pools in my underarms. Nausea foams in my gut.

The OldMill?!

"Just a second," I manage to say as I duck past him into the bathroom, ignoring the annoyed look on his face. Turning the cold water on full force, I soak my hand towel and use it to douse my face and the back of my neck in icy cold. The nausea subsides and I lie on the cold tile floor and breathe and count, like Dr. Crowchild taught me. How is this happening? A few hours ago, I was days away from getting my life back, and now I'm at a crossroads with an impossible choice: either help Dad work illegally for Nate, or tell Nate the truth about the fraud they hired. And if I choose the latter, what does that mean for me? All my hard work helping him get to this point will have been for nothing.

No. No, no, no. My nails cut into my palms. That can't happen. I can't keep doing this. I'm burning out. I need a way out. I want my life back. What. In. The. Actual. Heck. Is. Happening?

He knocks on the door. "Are you worried about the paperwork thing? Because it's not a big deal. I'm capable of doing plumbing work and I don't need a piece of paper that says so. This requirement that people see your certificates and diplomas to prove you're capable is ludicrous."

It's nothing I haven't heard him say before, and he's not wrong even though he is. I can't deny that he can be very capable. And if I keep my eyes and ears on the job he's doing, I can make sure that the work he does at the OldMill is honest and trustworthy. I know enough about how he works to know when he's cutting corners.

Getting up, I splash more cold water on my face, a plan taking shape in my mind. If I keep an eye on things, Nate and Dad can both get what they want, and I'll be free to get what I want too. Win. Win. Win.

Yes. It's the only way.

Slapping on my best smile, I open the door and agree to do what he wants. It always works to defuse things.

He smiles with his whole face. "I knew I could count on you, Lexie. I don't know what I'd do without you."

CHAPTER TWENTY

SATURDAY, MARCH 2

Nate's truck is resonating with the bass before we even lay eyes on the house.

"No doubt we're in the right area," he mutters.

"It's that house there, on the right," Zara says, pointing at a mansion-sized house at the end of a long driveway, flanked on either side by wrought iron light posts. A pair of huge pillars frame the double-wide front door, and based on how the bunch of people hanging out on the front steps with drinks in hand are dressed, it's obvious that they fit into this scene a lot better than I'm going to. One girl who looks familiar is hanging on the arm of one of the guys while she laughs at something that must have been hysterical, while another poses next to them, taking a selfie. I run my hand over my ponytail and I'm glad that Zara made us trial run our wardrobe two weeks ago.

Nate makes eye contact with me in his rearview mirror. I know this isn't his scene either, which makes the suffocating blanket of guilt I'm carrying around my shoulders feel even heavier. Since Dad started the renovations at the OldMill last week, I've felt like I should ask Nate how it's going, but I haven't been able to bring myself to do it, probably because I don't want to know.

"Are you sure about this, Zara?" I ask.

"Positive. Don't worry. We can't stay long anyway because I told my mom we'd be home by eleven."

The crowd on the porch doesn't look up when we walk past them into the enormous entry way. The gleaming white tile spreads in front of us like a road and the walls vibrate with the bass coming from the enormous speakers in the living room to the right. The room is bigger than Mom's entire house, and it's standing room only. The white leather furniture arranged in front of a stone fireplace is jammed with teenagers, the table in front of it littered with beer bottles, plastic cups, smashed pretzels, and bowls that have long been emptied of their chips. A grand piano is in the far corner. A guy and a girl sit squashed next to each other on its bench, laughing as they bang on it, pretending like they know what they're doing.

"Hey!" A girl with pink hair and heavily lined eyes yells over the noise from her perch on the end of one of the white leather sectionals. "You can't vape in here." She points to the back of the house. "Take it outside. My parents will kill me if they smell that in here."

"Zara!" A girl who must be Shayna shouts over the crowd.

"Beth!" Nope. Not Shayna. "I didn't know you were coming."

"Of course I was coming. Everybody who knows anybody's here."

"Is Shayna here? And Vanessa and Reah?"

"They're back there," she waves her hand, "watching a bunch of idiots play the foosball drinking game. Let's just say, it's getting pretty interesting. Come." She grabs Zara's hand. "We'll get drinks."

Zara looks back at us and does one of those jerks of her head that tells us to follow her, before she disappears into the throng of people lining the hall, pulled by Beth-not-Shayna.

Nate looks at me. I know what he's thinking. According to what he's told me, he was the undefeated foosball champion at his school. He's admitted that had he taken his classes as seriously as lunchtime foosball, his grades might've been a lot better.

We follow the sound of shouts and chants to the back of the house. Beyond the kitchen, down a short staircase, is another sitting room, also full of teenagers, many of them dancing to Dua Lipa's "Levitating." On the other side of the room, an intense game of foosball is being played. Two guys are on each side of the table, all four in deep concentration working the rods, while a bunch of spectators jump around, shouting encouragement. A girl stands on a chair behind them, filming the crazy with her phone. At that moment the game stops, a cheer goes up, and the losing team and their supporters chug back a plastic cup of beer.

"I need to get in on that action, minus the beer," Nate says. "You know any of those guys? Maybe introduce me?"

I shake my head. "No. But I think Zara —"

"Lexie, how's it going? I haven't seen you at practice in a while. Is it true that you quit swim?"

Turning, I'm surprised to see Derek, the kid who works maintenance at the pool. Nate looks at me, his eyes splayed wide.

"What? No. Why would you think that?"

He shrugs. "Just a rumor. And since I haven't seen you at practice in forever, I thought maybe it was true."

"No. I've just been busy with other stuff. I'll be back at practice soon."

"Don't wait too long. I'm sure you've heard that the competition's heating up."

"What do you mean?"

"Ridgeview's team picked up a new swimmer. Charlotte something or other. She can butterfly like a champ."

His news rattles me, more than I want to admit. It could mean my scholarship's at risk.

I wave my hand. "I'm not worried. I've been in the pool, just on off hours, so that's why you haven't seen me."

Lie.

"Your homework this week is to do something for yourself."

A cheer and a groan erupt from the foosball crowd, while at the same time Zara yells at me, waving me over from the kitchen. Nate lifts his chin at Derek. "You think you could get me in on that?"

"For sure. You play?"

"Used to."

"You any good?"

Nate smiles. "I'm not bad."

"Sweet. Follow me."

Nate shoots me a playful wink. "I'll find you later."

I pick my way across the room, dodging groups of people and a couple going at it in the corner. Bits of Cheez-Its crunch under my feet as I go. Plastic cups, half-empty two-fours, and Smirnoff bottles are strewn across the kitchen's island. At least the kitchen is a little less crowded with the exception of the bunch of people standing around the keg, positioned beside the sink.

"Lexie," says Zara. "This is Shayna, Beth, Trish, Vanessa, and Reah. They're all on council with me."

"Hi," I say, my stomach twisting on a knot. I twirl my ponytail around my finger.

"Your hand's empty," says Shayna. "Let's fix that."

She holds a plastic cup under the keg and then hands it to me, the warm beer splashes over the side. I don't want it. I hate beer. Tastes like dirty dishwater, although I admit I haven't tasted dirty dishwater. That's just what I expect it would taste like. Zara's got one in her hand too, but I know she's not drinking it. I don't want to seem rude or ungrateful though, so I sip at it. Yup. Dirty dishwater.

"Hey," the girl who I think is Reah says. "Are you the Lexie that's dating Rhys?"

I feel my face flush. "We've gone out a few times."

"You're so lucky. He's super hot."

"Yeah," adds Vanessa. "I'd do him."

"Vanessa!"

"What? I'm just being honest."

Reah shakes her head. "Ignore her. She's had one too many. Where is he? I thought this was his scene."

"He had to work," I say.

"You sure about that?" Shayna asks, her eyes glued on something behind me. "Because that looks like him over there, and he doesn't look happy."

"You cheated!" Rhys yells, flinging his hand off the rod. "Who is this guy anyway?"

Zara's eyes grow wide. "Is he yelling at Nate?"

"Rhys, dude," says Derek from his position atop one of the barstools. "He wasn't cheating. That was a legit game."

What the heck? Why didn't he tell me he was coming?

My resident butterflies start fanning my insides on cue as I dodge around people, back to the games room.

"Nah man." Nate's voice. "I don't cheat. You just don't like losing."

A chorus of "ooooh" goes through the crowd.

Zara, as usual, gets through the crowd faster than me. I'm okay with it. I'm happy to let her make the necessary introductions and defuse the situation. I don't think I could anyway. My butterflies have climbed up my throat. This isn't how I wanted Rhys and Nate to meet each other. I'd tried a couple times to get Rhys to pick me up at the marina, or come by so I could introduce him to Nate, but he said he hardly ever got to see me, so when he did, he didn't want to use the little time we had together with other people. Which is sweet, I think, because it proves that he does want to be with me.

Zara sidles up next to Nate. "Rhys, meet Nate. He was his high school's undefeated foosball champion. Nate, meet Rhys." Her hand waves back and forth between the two as she makes the necessary introductions.

An awkward silence goes by as Zara's introduction sinks in. I try to ignore the look of disapproval on Nate's face, pretend it doesn't bother me. Rhys's pissed-off look changes to one of recognition and his eyes scan around, finally land on mine.

"I would've introduced you guys, had I known you were coming," I say.

He comes around the table and takes my hand before he kisses my hair. "I switched my shift. I sent you a text."

I pull out my phone and scroll through it, looking for what I missed. Everyone's looking at me and my face gets hot. I feel like a fish in a bowl.

Nate rescues me. "Lexie's told me a lot about you."

His eye catches mine, and his unasked questions float between us before mine dart away, because it's a lie. I haven't told him anything. He only knows what Zara told him when she blabbed about him one day on one of our FT calls.

Rhys nods at him, and they continue to look each other up and down, like they're trying to identify the other's weak spots.

"Well, *this* is awkward!" Derek announces from his position on the barstool. "Who else wants a go against Nate the foosball champion?"

An hour, a headache, and two Jell-O shots later, I find Nate alone on the back deck.

"I've been looking all over for you."

From outside, the intensity of the music and drunken singing to Ed Sheeran's "Shape of You" is muted, but it still makes the lump of blue Jell-O in the bottom of my Dixie Cup jiggle. It's the third one Rhys has handed me in the last hour, and based on the fact that my head feels disconnected from my body, I don't think I should do another. I'd learned the hard way once and ended up with my head in the toilet. I'd like to say that I learned from that experience and have no intention of doing that again.

"I needed a break from that," he says, his thumb hitching at the house behind us.

"Me too. Want this?" I ask, offering him the Dixie Cup. He gives me a look. "Didn't think so." I tip the cup over the railing, watch the blue cube slide out and bounce off the bushes, landing in the snow-covered garden beneath. "Are you still the undefeated champion?"

"Totally." He kicks at the ice along the bottom of the railing. "I don't think your boyfriend appreciated it, though."

"It's not like that. You took him by surprise. I don't think he was expecting a champion foosball player, or that said champion would be his girlfriend's guy friend."

"You're probably right. Where is he anyway? It seemed like he had a good grip on your hand."

I pretend to not notice what I'm pretty sure is criticism.

"He went to find me some water. My headache tells me it's necessary."

I shiver, pull my jacket tighter around me, and argue with myself about whether I should ask him what I want to know, but don't want to know. I decide my need to know mostly outweighs my preference to not know.

"How's the renovation going?"

His shoulder bounces. "Seems okay so far."

My blanket of guilt instantly eases, making me stumble forward.

I'm doing the right thing. I made the right decision. Everyone will get what they need.

Nate catches my elbow. "Whoa. How many drinks have you had?"

I laugh and look up at him, and the way he searches my eyes, like he can see inside me, makes my stomach hitch in a weird way.

"No more foosball for you?" Rhys sticks his hand between us to give me a plastic cup. Nate drops my elbow and steps to the side, making room for Rhys to wedge himself between us.

"There wasn't anyone left to play against," Nate says. "Want to have another go?"

"I'm good, thanks." Rhys puts his arm around me, pulling me close, but despite being outside, the air around us feels thick and tight, almost claustrophobic.

I want to kick myself. The weirdness between them could've been avoided if I'd made sure they met properly, rather than over testosterone, beer, and foosball. I take a sip from the cup Rhys handed me and gag. It's syrupy sweet, spiked with something cheap. "What is this?"

"You like it?" Rhys asks.

"I asked for water."

"I know. But I thought you'd like that better."

The glare Nate gives Rhys could cut glass, and my butterflies get in line. He opens his mouth to say something, but at that moment, the muted thumping from inside amplifies when Zara steps out, and he doesn't. I sag a little with relief and hope they don't notice.

"I've been looking for you two everywhere. We have to go. And Nate, you need to move your car, pronto. Someone's stuck in the snow and it's in the way."

"On it," he says. His eyes linger on mine for a longer-than-normal moment before he darts past Zara into the house.

"Lexie, you coming?" she asks.

"Just give me two minutes."

It's finally quiet, just the two of us and the distant thumping from inside. He wraps his arms around me from behind and nuzzles into my neck. "You're not actually leaving now, are you?" he asks, his lips against my ear.

"I have to. I'm staying at Zara's tonight. My mom's covering a night shift."

He pulls away and spins me around to face him. A smile

spreads over his face. “I’ve got a better idea. We can sneak away for a bit. Go to our spot. It’s the perfect opportunity since your mom’s not expecting you home.”

I laugh, figuring he’s joking. “I can’t do that.”

His smile slips off his face. “Why not?”

I look at him, try to judge whether or not he’s serious. “I can’t ditch Zara.”

“You’d rather hang out with her than me?”

His words drop from his lips like stones, their weight practically makes divots in the snow. My breath sticks in my throat and I lean farther away from him, the railing digging into my back.

“No. It’s just that —”

“We haven’t seen each other — like *seen* each other — in ages. You see her all the time. You’re neighbors.” He leans down and kisses me.

It’s not true. We’ve seen each other despite the fact that I’ve missed swim. He’s been coming to Dad’s a couple of nights a week, and I’ve been going to the park with Mav to meet him there.

“Please? She’s your best friend. If she cared about you, she’d want you to do what you want.”

My skin turns clammy and my stupid butterflies slap at my insides again. How does this always happen? Why does it feel like no matter what I do, I’m always caught in the middle?

He rests his forehead on mine. “Please? For me?”

I can’t let him think that Zara’s more important to me than he is, and while she might be annoyed at first, she’ll understand that this is necessary.

“Okay,” I whisper.

He smiles and tilts his head down, allowing his lips to brush mine, much like they did the first time on the path, and I know things are okay between us. I return his kiss, letting him know that I can be the girlfriend he wants me to be. My stomach flutters again, but this time it's my butterflies trying to lift me up, rather than drag me down.

I find Zara digging through the pile of jackets someone tossed behind the couch.

"Reah and Vanessa are coming to crash at my place too. It'll be great. An all-night gossip and *Bachelor* fest."

Relief washes through me that Zara's post-party sleepover isn't going to go completely belly up because my plans have changed.

"That's great. Mind if I join you guys a bit later?"

She freezes and turns to face me. "Why?"

"Rhys wants me to go with him. He can drop me at your place in a couple of hours."

"But *we* have plans."

"I know. But Rhys wants —"

A pair of hands settle on my hips and Zara's expression sours. The butterflies that were dancing with airy leaps moments ago are now clumsy and heavy, bumping all over each other.

"You ready?"

Zara's disapproving glare is burning a hole in the side of my head. "Lexie and I have plans. You know that, right, Rhys?"

"You guys always have plans. You won't mind if I borrow your bestie for a couple of hours, will you?"

"Actually, I do mind," she says.

His arm snakes around my waist and I feel his spine lengthen. They stare at each other, a silent duel, like I'm not even there. I feel like one of Mav's tug toys, each of them pulling me in opposite directions.

"I guess it's up to Lexie then," Rhys says, bending to kiss the side of my head. "I'm fine with whatever."

The pit in my stomach is a cavern and my butterflies are giant flapping warty toads. There's something about the way he says "fine with whatever" that makes me think he won't be "fine with whatever." But then he smiles the smile that makes me melt, and I think I probably imagined it. It's obvious though that Zara won't be "fine with whatever," and I'm irritated that she can't be a little more understanding. It's a no-win situation. If I go with Rhys, Zara will be mad, but she's got Reah and Vanessa to keep her company till I get there. But if I say no to Rhys, he'll think I'd rather hang with my friends than him, which isn't true. At least not always. And since Rhys is my boyfriend, he takes priority, doesn't he? Shouldn't he? And shouldn't Zara, as my BFF, just get that I have to put him first? She would if it were her, wouldn't she? Wouldn't anyone? She's also been opinionated about Rhys lately, entertaining all kinds of rumors, which is getting on my nerves. She was the one who said she was going to live vicariously through me, so why can't she be happy for me?

I try again. "What if —"

Suddenly Rhys's arm around my waist is a bit too tight and it feels like I'm being smothered. I try to step away from his grip, but he holds tight, like he owns me.

"I won't be long," I say. "He'll drop me at your place later. That way I can do both."

I look between them, hoping that my solution appeases both of them. I'm usually very good at fixing things so everyone's happy.

A hint of sadness floats across Zara's eyes before it's replaced with anger. "Don't bother. It's obvious you'd rather be with your boyfriend than me."

I sigh. "Zara, what do you expect me to do?"

"I'll pull the car up front," Rhys murmurs in my ear, before disappearing.

"For starters, I'd expect that instead of changing our plans, you'd make plans with your boyfriend for next weekend. He wasn't even planning to come tonight, and now he's desperate to be with you? Not to mention he has a problem with Nate, and he lied about texting you."

"He didn't lie. I must have been out of range. And he doesn't have a problem with Nate. If I'd been able to introduce them —"

She scoffs a laugh. "Would you listen to yourself? You're making excuses for him. When are you going to open your eyes?"

"They are open, Zara. I guess we see different things."

"No argument there." She shakes her head. "We used to be on the same page, but now it's like you're in a different book. The Lexie I know wouldn't ditch me for a guy. That's got to tell you something about your boyfriend."

I stare at her, hurt and anger bubbling to the surface. "Forget it. Have fun with Vanessa and Reah. I'm not coming."

"Good," she says, turning back to the pile of jackets.

I turn to leave, but when I glance back before I slip out the door, I'm surprised to see her wiping her eyes.

We're in the back seat of his car, parked in our spot under the willow overlooking the lake, and he's kissing me harder than usual. His tongue, usually soft and delicate, is stabbing the inside of my mouth, moving too fast, like it's searching for something. I'm not sure I like this new frenzied way of making out, but I try to concentrate on how lucky I am that it's me he wants, when I know he can have any girl. When his lips move away from my mouth to trail down the length of my neck, I take the chance to gather some space, take a breath.

"What's wrong?" he asks.

I rub my swollen lip. "Nothing."

"It's Zara, isn't it?" He pulls away, holds my eyes with his.

"I knew she'd be mad."

"She's being selfish, expecting you to do what she wants."

"You think so?"

"For sure. It was all about her and what she wanted."

I think maybe he's right. She wasn't willing to hear me out at all.

"Has she always been like that?"

"Like what?"

"I don't know. Snobby. Controlling."

I flinch. While I'm annoyed at her right now, I know she wasn't trying to be controlling. She hates it when her carefully made plans go awry. But the fact that she couldn't meet me half-way, that she couldn't compromise with me, *is* selfish. Why haven't I seen that before?

"Enough about her, though," he says, brushing my ponytail off my shoulder. "You're with me now."

"You're right. No more talk about Zara."

"Good," he says, nuzzling my earlobe.

A wave of shivers runs down my spine, making me giggle. "But what's up with your foosball friend?"

I pull away. "What do you mean?"

"Have you guys ever had a thing?"

"You mean, have we ever been together, like as a couple?"

"Yeah. That."

"No. Never going to happen."

"Does he feel that way too?"

"Definitely. I've known him since I moved here. We're good friends and we work together, but that's it."

One of his eyebrows lifts higher than the other. "Are you sure about that? Because it's obvious he's into you. He was clinging to your arm, like he was trying to pull you into him. I don't know how you don't see it."

I don't know what to say to that. Does Nate think that way about me? My thoughts about it don't much matter though, because Rhys's hands have snaked up the inside of my shirt and unhooked my bra. His left hand is now kneading my boob, sending shock waves through my body. I hear myself gasp, which I guess he interprets as pleasure, because it makes him squeeze harder while the fingers of his right hand make their way down the waistband of my tights. A panic rises up in me that I fight, desperate to shove back in its box before it ruins my chance with the best thing that's ever happened to me. The regular me wants to tell him that he's moving too fast, that I'm not comfortable with the journey his hands are making under my clothes, touching the places only I've touched. But I don't let her say anything. If I let her speak, she'll screw this up. Screw us up. He'll think I'm rejecting him, and he already thinks I'm too close to Nate, so that can't happen. It'll be the end of us and we're only getting started.

"You're okay with this, right?"

No. No, I'm not. Stop. Please stop.

"Of course," I say, kissing him harder, giving his hands free license to go into all my places. I'm not going to ruin things by worrying and overthinking like I always do. I need to prove to him that he's the one I want, be the girl he thinks I am.

"Why are you always making mountains out of molehills, Lexie? You're just like your mother. Can't you just relax and stop being so difficult?"

So I let him lead the way, and ignore the voice inside me that's always looking for problems where there aren't any. The voice that's telling me to make him stop. That it's too much too fast. That I don't want his fingers creeping that far up the crease between my thighs.

You know you can say no. You don't have to do anything you don't want to.

Shut up, stupid brain. Shut up. Don't ruin this for me.

My heart stutters, jumps around in concert with my butterflies, but I'm pretty sure they're the good kind. Like the way people describe their heart racing when they fall in love. Like in the movies and romance novels.

After, when we're done, he drops me off at the empty house. In bed, I pull the covers up to my neck and curl into a ball, but those damn butterflies won't stay still. I squeeze my eyes shut and count and breathe, count and breathe. I did what I had to, didn't I? How else could I prove to Rhys that he's important to me? But I stay awake all night.

CHAPTER TWENTY-ONE

MONDAY, MARCH 11

It's in my email, arrived two hours ago at 4:46 p.m. It's from the Sunridge admissions office. The subject of the email gives nothing away. It says: "Re: Your application to the School of Fine Art and Music." My butterflies awaken and start their sickly rubbing of my insides. They're always there lately, the ones that make me feel queasy and make me sweat in uncomfortable places.

I know Mom will want to know what it says, but she's not home yet. She was here after work at her regular job to make dinner, but now she's out at her other job. It's been our new normal since Dad quit his day job. She still doesn't know about that though. Another secret I wish I didn't know and would rather not keep. She said she needed the second job to pay for all the extra stuff, like my swim club dues. I died a little inside when she said that. I know I didn't help things when I tricked her into giving me two hundred dollars for nonexistent swim club dues so that she could pay for necessities for the dog she doesn't have. I remind myself that I didn't have a choice. That I did what I had to do to keep everyone happy. That I needed to make sure Mav was taken care of. I'll pay her back, eventually, somehow.

I stare at the email, bold and unread in my inbox. It might as well be written in all caps, flashing at me in neon, excited emojis everywhere, it's so loud in my face. This is it. The moment I've been hoping for and dreading at the same time. If it's a rejection email, I'll be devastated. But if I'm accepted, then the metaphorical boat has officially set sail, no putting it off any longer. I'll have to tell him that I'm switching schools. That I won't have time to help him with his business anymore. My stomach lurches. If it's an acceptance, it's my way out.

"You're allowed to set your own goals for yourself. You can't be everything to everybody."

I check my phone to see if Zara's texted. Of course she hasn't. We'd promised each other that we'd be together when we opened the emails, but she still won't talk to me, even though I've sent her about forty-seven hundred messages apologizing and trying to explain. Even though I don't think it's my fault. At least, not entirely. She's been avoiding me at practice too, and the other day when I was standing at the bus stop, she looked right through me when she drove by with her dad. There was no way she didn't see me. That hurt. I release a breath I didn't know I was holding and grab at my stomach, willing the damn butterflies to go away. I squeeze my eyes shut and count and breathe, count and breathe, before I grab my phone and head out the door. I can't be alone when I open it.

Nate's bent over a life-size cardboard rendition of Gertrude. I watch through the window as he uses bright yellow paint to draw a large letter *G* on the back of our hopefully unsinkable, but likely very sinkable, cardboard boat. The plan is that I'll take the front, and he'll steer from the back.

Next to cardboard Gertrude, shoved against the shop wall and propped on a boat rack, is Dad's boat. We haven't had a chance to work on it much since Pops died. Not with all the stuff that's keeping both Nate and me busy. I should be able to get back to it soon, though. A few guys responded to the help wanted ad I posted online. Some of the résumés look promising, so it shouldn't be long before Dad hires someone, which will free me up to get back to my regular things, including finishing his boat.

Nate looks up at the sound of the door creaking open, tosses his fringe of hair out of his eyes. His grin slides off his face. "What's up with you? Why do you look like somebody died?"

I force my lips into something that'll pass as a smile. "I got an email from Sunridge."

"Okay," he says, like it's a question.

"I'm nervous to open it. What if I got in?"

"Isn't that what you've been gunning for?"

"Yes, but — here." I hand him my phone. "Can you just read it for me, tell me what it says?"

He takes it from me, his look of confusion now mixed with concern. I pretend not to notice and turn away from him.

"You're in, Lexie," he says. The pride in his voice is loud. "You did it."

Relief floods through me, as does a renewed anxiety that makes my legs feel mushy. I grab the boat rack to steady myself.

He hands me my phone, searches my face. "Aren't you happy about this?"

"Yes. It's just —"

It's just my dad's not going to like it, and now there's this whole other thing with him and you that you don't even know about that could go really, really badly, and Zara still won't talk to me.

"It's just Zara and I were supposed to be together when we got the news, but she's taking this thing that happened with Rhys way too far. It wasn't that big of a deal."

A frown etches at the corners of his mouth.

"Why are you looking at me like that? Did she tell you something?"

He doesn't miss a beat. "It is a big deal, Lexie. It's an even bigger deal that you don't see it."

Heat roars up the back of my neck, slapping my cheeks with warmth. "Don't see what?"

He tilts his head to the side, like he can't believe he has to spell it out for me. "Your boyfriend's a walking red flag."

All my worries about Dad and Sunridge disappear and I pin my arms over my chest, return his look with a glare. He's got it all wrong. Just like Zara, he's reading everything all wrong.

"He hovered over you like he owned you. He brought you alcohol when you asked for water, he had no issue disrespecting me, and he guilted you into ditching your plans with Zara."

"Is that what she told you?"

"It's what happened, isn't it?" Air huffs from his nostrils. "Look. I didn't want to get into this with you. This is between you and Zara and … him. I just think —"

"What do you think?"

"Red flags, Lexie. They're not always about other people."

I blink at him, waiting for him to explain. I have no idea what that means.

His gaze drills into mine, concern mixed with empathy, and a weird, edgy feeling comes over me, like he knows something I don't.

"When you change the things you do because you're scared of the way someone will react, that's the red flag you need to pay attention to."

CHAPTER TWENTY-TWO

THURSDAY, MARCH 14

We're sitting in a booth, kitty-corner to the bar. Every seat in the place is taken, all eyes except mine are glued to one of the flat-screen TVs, watching the Leafs battle the Montréal Canadiens. I've been scrolling through my phone. Servers squeeze past each other balancing plates piled high with nachos and fries, big wooden bowls of all-you-can-eat salad, and sizzling fajitas, while bartenders pass out drinks along the packed bar, and stack drinks on trays while they yell orders back and forth. Above my head, a chalkboard sign lists today's specials: roasted cream of tomato soup with house-made garlic croutons, blackened chili-lime salmon with rice and mango salsa, and double-chocolate lava mudslide with raspberry coulis for dessert.

I have to admit that my stomach grumbles at all the delectable smells. And it's nice to just sit and be served.

I was supposed to be visiting Mr. Harris tonight, but Dad called the nursing home and said I was sick. He said, "You're always complaining that you've got too much to do. This is your time to relax. A special family dinner."

A server hovers over our table. "I've got a double-decker burger with extra cheese and bacon —"

"Right here," Jonah says, rubbing his hands together.

"And I have an extreme burger with extra guac and a side of onion rings —"

"That's mine," says Dad.

"— and, last but not least, gluten-free linguine with herb-garlic chicken." She slides my plate in front of me. It looks and smells delicious. I set my phone down on the bench beside me and pull the plate closer.

"Anything else I can get you folks?" Her name tag says Jen and she looks like an older version of Sophie Turner.

Dad orders another beer, Jonah a Coke, and I get a Perrier.

"Be right back," Jen says, tucking her notepad and pen in her front smock.

"You know that's not a real thing, right?" Dad says, gesturing toward my plate.

"What?"

"The whole gluten-free thing. The restaurant industry just made it up so they could put another more expensive option on their menu. It's crazy how many idiots buy into it."

I sigh inside. I've known for three years now that I'm gluten intolerant. Mom sent Dad the doctor's report, and I've told him a bazillion times that when I eat gluten, I feel sick. I'm about to explain it again, the way the doctor explained it to me, but Jen returns with our drinks, so I let it go.

"Anything else I can get for you?" she asks.

"We're good," Dad says.

"Enjoy." She drops some extra napkins on the table and turns to the people at the table next to us.

"What are we celebrating?" I ask. "Did you hire that Chris guy? His résumé looked good."

"No. We didn't like him much," Jonah says, sipping his Coke.

"Why?"

Jonah plays it up, loving the fact that I'm hanging on his every word. "He wasn't the right fit for us. Right, Dad?"

"But on paper, he was everything you needed," I say.

"Except in person he was a bit of a dick," Dad quips back. "He was a know-it-all, wasn't he, Jonah?"

Jonah's head bobs. "Yup. He looked at the plumbing Dad did, and told him he used the wrong drain fittings, which is total bull crap, because you can use tees or wyes, right, Dad?"

Dad slaps Jonah on the back. "That's right, bud. There's nothing wrong with the way I did it. That guy just wanted to show me up."

I force myself to swallow over the lump of uneasiness that's brewing in my throat. The perfect candidate showed up for the job, a guy who has a legitimate plumber's license, and Dad didn't like his professional opinion? "So who got the job, then?"

They share a look and a sly smile, and a weird slippery feeling slips down my spine. I sip at my Perrier, try to force a calm in me. The bubbles are sharp on my tongue.

"Go ahead. Tell her," Dad says.

"Us!" Jonah blurts out.

My heart kicks into overdrive, and my butterflies scratch my insides with their sharp wings.

No. This can't be what he's decided. This is not what we agreed on.

Dad's voice is far away. Echoey, like he's in a tunnel. The hum of conversation around us dulls and washes out while the clattering sound of plates and glasses being stacked behind the bar gets sharper, making my ears ring. It's at this moment that I wake up to the reality I was pretending didn't exist. He never had any intention of hiring Chris — or anyone, for that matter. Jonah and I were his plan all along. The *Family* Business.

"It's what's best for the business." Dad's voice cuts through the ringing. "It's come so far already, so I don't see why it can't continue like this. Why hire an outsider to mess things up? You know what they say: If it ain't broke, don't fix it."

Jonah's head bobs as he takes big gulps of his Coke. As usual, he's agreeing with everything Dad says.

"What do you think, Lexie? It's a good idea, isn't it?"

"It's just for a bit longer, Lexie. I promise. Just till I can afford to hire someone."

"It's not selfish to choose yourself, Lexie."

Ignoring the voice of the me I don't want to be anymore, the one that's begging me to keep my mouth shut, I say, "No. This wasn't the deal. You said that us helping was temporary. Until you could hire outside help. Then you wouldn't need us anymore."

The air in our booth stills and his smile slips, like it was a fake stick-on one, and I see his real self peek out from underneath. The slippery feeling is back, and that's when I know for sure nothing I do will be enough. It'll never be enough. He doesn't care about my opinion, or anything important to me. He never has.

And now that I've dared to disagree, I've erased all the work I've done trying to prove that I'm someone I'm not, so that I can start being the someone I am. If anything's become clear over the past few months, it's that I can't be both. Again, I have to choose to let someone down, and this time it's not going to be me.

His eyes take on a stark darkness. "I never said that. I proposed starting a family business and you agreed to help with it.

Promised me and Jonah that we had your full support. I said we *might* be able to hire someone in the future."

My mind scrambles, my muscles tense. He didn't say "might." He said he planned on hiring someone else. I know he did. I know because I finally rescued that darn journal from the bottom of my bag and wrote it down. I've read it dozens of times. I know what he said. He can't just change what he said then to make it suit what he wants now.

Normally this would be the point at which I'd give in to his demands before things spiral too far down a path I can't come back from, but I can't bring myself to do it this time. I won't.

"I'm going to Sunridge in the fall. Their art program. I applied and got accepted." I throw my words out so they'll sound strong and triumphant, try to convince myself of confidence I don't have.

He scowls, like he's seeing something he's never seen before. The silence screeches of disappointment, and I pedal backward, trying to salvage at least a bit of what I just broke.

"I should've told you about my plans, but I wanted to make sure your business was okay first."

I keep talking, tripping over my words, try to crack his icy stare. I tell myself to shut up, but my mouth doesn't listen. It keeps talking, like a boat motor with no shut-off valve, saying more stuff I want him to know, even though most of me knows he doesn't care.

"And I was hoping that you'd …"

He leans closer to me, his eyes pools of emptiness. I lean back, but the wall of the booth prevents me from stealing more space for myself.

"That I'd what?"

"That you'd be happy for me. That you'd be proud of me. Now that I've spent so much time helping you, I hoped you'd let me do something that's important to me."

My words fall over themselves, piling up on the table in front of me. Even though I know they're the words that need to be said, it's like my tongue knows they're unforgivable, and tries to hold them back. I want to pick them up, rearrange them into something he'll approve of.

If his words were liquid, I'd be able to catch the contempt that dripped from them. "Proud of you? You applied to transfer to a school in her district and you didn't tell me. That's called lying, Lexie."

His eyebrows squish together and his head tilts to the side. "This was her idea, wasn't it? Never mind that you're backing out on your promise to me and Jonah."

No I'm not. I'm pretty certain I didn't make any such promise.

"Did you ever stop to think about me? How you going to that school will make my life harder?" His face is red and his nostrils flare. "It'll be your fault if our business falls apart, because you were too busy with yourself. And where will that leave me?"

His accusations kick me in the stomach.

"Sunridge is something I need to do for me," I say it again, and I hate that it sounds like I'm begging. Why do I need to beg to be who I want to be?

He rolls his eyes and throws up his hands. "Well! Big surprise. Lexie's thinking about herself again. Me. Me. Me. That's all you ever think about. You sound just like her. So selfish."

I sit on my hands to steady my tremor, and count and breathe, count and breathe, searching the depths of me for another ounce of courage. How could I have been so stupid to think that he'd see me and what I want, the same way I saw him?

"You know what?" He leans over the table, his eyes a pointy glare. "I'm not going to argue with you. You will decline the offer to that school, since you didn't have my permission to apply in the first place."

Heat spreads up the back of my neck and swells across my scalp, making it prickle. "No," I say, surprising myself with the sound of my strength. "I'm going to Sunridge. I worked hard to get in, and I deserve to do what I want to do for me, like I helped you do what you wanted to do, for you."

His open palms slam against the table. People turn to stare at us.

"It doesn't matter what *you* want," he yells, his finger stabbing the air in front of my face, "because you're the child and I'm the parent, and you do what *I* say."

He goes on and on and I curl into myself, feel cemented in place, unable to move.

"And what about Maverick? I got you that dog, the one you begged me for. Have you thought about who's going to take care of him while you're busy at that other school, on *her* side of town?" His mouth twitches then, giving him away. "We both know that you can't depend on Jonah and me to do it. The poor dog needs you."

Vomit rises in the back of my throat. That's why he got Maverick? A tether to his house and his bidding. My skin goes clammy; I'm fuming and shocked at the same time, and I can't isolate one feeling from the other.

"How are we doing here?" Jen the waitress jars me back to reality. "Can I take those plates away for you? Wrap up the leftovers?"

I feel my head nod, hand her my plate of untouched food.

"I'll be right back with the dessert menu."

He looks at me, his eyes filled with hurt, and I can't help feeling the blanket of blame he places on me. "After all I've done for you, I can't believe you'd stab me in the back like this." He shakes his head, his lips a disapproving thin line. "I'm so disappointed in you."

The words slam into me, steal my breath, carve themselves into my brain so I don't forget.

"I'm so disappointed in you."

Jen's back, at my side. "Our dessert special is our homemade double-chocolate lava mudslide with raspberry coulis."

I can't do this. I need to get out of here. I mumble something about needing to go to the bathroom and slide out of the booth as Jen lays out clean plates and forks and tops up our water glasses. Despite the hot, angry tears that blur my vision, the truth I've been avoiding for so long cuts deep, leaving a scar so I'll never forget. I walk past the bar and head down the hall. At the end is a heavy metal door propped open to the outside with a block of wood. I make a decision then, as I walk past the bathroom and step out the door into the parking lot and the cold night. I don't know where I'm going, but it has to be far away from here, far away from him. The only thing I know for sure is that I'm done trying to be someone I'm not.

I will my legs to move faster, tripping over the uneven sidewalk while the tears I refused to give him chase each other down my cheeks. Glancing over my shoulder to make sure they're not following me, I break into a run, dart left down an alleyway and around the corner, increasing the distance between me and him. I pass the park that Mom always used to take us to, where I've been taking Mav to play fetch just about every day before and after school, flee through the shadows of the trees. Normally I admire their majestic arms, the way they seem to hold up the sky, but tonight, in the cold dark sky void of its stars, it's like they're pointing their branches down at me, their twisty arms accusing, and I cross to the other side, where they can't reach me.

"After all I've done for you."

I keep going, one foot in front of the other, tears gumming up the back of my throat, until I feel I'm far enough away that they won't find me. That's when I bend forward, hands on my knees, and retch into the dirt. Vomit made of anger, hope, disappointment, and grief splashes up onto the side of a tree. I stand with my head bowed, hands on my knees, breathing and counting before I step away and keep walking, farther away from the restaurant, from his house, from my life with him, wiping the river of tears that won't stop. I don't know how long I've been walking — minutes? hours? — before my bones rattle and I realize that I left my jacket behind. Spying an empty bus shelter on the opposite side of the street, I sit on the icy metal bench and wrap my arms tight around my calves, rest my forehead on my knees. Cold shudders through me. Happy memories of better, easier times with Dad come at me in pieces, but the last thing he said to me erases it all. Taints it. Like tarnished brass.

"I'm so disappointed in you."

Reality has hit me like a fist; a truth I can no longer deny is clear. Dad's not the dad he's been pretending to be. His realness is the one that made that awful slippery feeling slide down my spine.

A bus screeches to a halt in front of me. The doors swish open and warm air spills out, beckoning me. My body's numb, and my face is sticky from tears. I know I must look awful, but I don't care. I uncurl my frozen legs from the bench and climb on. I don't care where it's going. It doesn't matter.

The bus lurches to a stop, jerking me awake. I blink against the stark white light, try to get my bearings.

"Last stop," the driver announces, only to me. He watches from the rearview mirror as I get up from my seat and reach into my pocket. My phone's not there. And then I remember setting it on the bench beside me at the restaurant. Damn.

"You need me to call someone for you?"

My eyes fill with tears. "Could you call my mom?"

He plugs in the number and hands me his phone.

She answers on the first ring.

"It's me."

"Where are you, are you okay?"

My throat coats with tears again. "I'm fine. I'm at the bus station. Can you come get me?"

When I got in the car, Mom's eyes swam with a million questions but the only one she asked was if I wanted to talk. I told her I didn't. She didn't push, and we drove home to the sound of the wipers wiping away the misty fog that was rolling along the ground. It was like it was chasing me, wanting to hold me down, to keep what I now see from being exposed. My feeling of quiet relief, though, disappears when we turn onto our street. There's a police car parked in front of the house. Bile rises in the back of my throat.

"What's going on? Why is there a cop here?"

I ask the question, even though I know the answer. I know they're here for me, that Dad sent them. It's something he would do.

Even though Mom's voice is unwavering, and despite the darkness cloaking the car, I sense her tension.

"I don't know. Maybe they're here for one of the neighbors."

"What're we going to do?" I ask, panic climbing up my throat. But then I remember that I didn't do anything wrong, and I try to focus on that.

"Nothing," she says, rolling past the cop car and turning into our driveway. "I didn't call them, and we haven't done anything wrong — or is there something you need to tell me?"

"What? No!"

She puts the car in park and takes off her seat belt. "Then I'm going to assume they're not here for us, and I'm going inside. Coming?"

I follow her lead, forcing myself to not look at the cop car and follow her inside. She's barely closed the door when the doorbell rings. I throw up a little in my mouth.

"Take it easy," Mom says to me as she opens the door again.

The officer flashes his badge. "Ms. Moore?"

"Yes," Mom says, but she says it like a question, rather than an affirmation of fact.

"I'm Officer DeBrun. I'm here at the request of your husband —"

"Ex-husband."

"Ex-husband, sorry, to conduct a welfare check on" — he flips through his notepad — "Lexie. Your ex-husband claims he's been unable to make contact with her, and that she's court mandated to be in his care today."

My head snaps up. *What the heck? What am I, four years old?*

His gaze slides to me. "Are you Lexie?"

I don't answer.

"This is Lexie, yes," says Mom. "And I notified her father that I'd located her, and that she was safe, so I'm not sure why he felt the need to call you."

"Well, he did, and it's my job to follow it up." His eyes trap mine. "Did you walk away from Weezie's restaurant earlier this evening?"

I nod.

"But before you left, you made a comment referencing your desire to end your life."

"What?! No I didn't!" My blood gets hot, making me tremble, and a buzzing starts in my ears, like a nest of angry hornets has been released. "I said I was going to the bathroom but left out the back door. My father lied to you."

The officer's expression doesn't change.

"Did you give him some reason to believe —"

"No. I didn't."

"So, you have no intention of hurting yourself?"

"No. I never did."

He nods. Does he believe me? "I'll be in touch with him to let him know you're safe, and I urge you to do the same."

I just look at him. I refuse to answer his non-question.

"Since you're under your father's care today, you should consider returning there tonight."

I stiffen. "I'm not going back there."

His eyes land on Mom. "I encourage you to follow the access schedule that you and your ex-husband agreed on. It makes things easier on everyone if everybody follows the rules."

Words come at me all at once from every direction, crash into each other, break apart, and fall away. No. Just no.

"In my experience," he continues, "kids and parents get into arguments all the time. Even if he's wrong, he is your dad. I'm sure he just wants what's best for you."

Pain radiates through my tongue and I struggle to not gag on the coppery taste that floods my mouth. Dad's mask must've been on nice and tight when Officer Clueless spoke to him, but that's no surprise. Dad's mask is always on when he's outside of the house. How do I make this police officer, a normal, regular person, understand that things aren't the way Dad frames them? I know how it'll sound if I try: I'll look like a crazy teenager while he looks the picture of a concerned father, the victim of his unruly teenage daughter. Exactly the picture he painted.

"Thank you, officer," Mom says. "We'll be in touch with Lexie's father and work this out."

Then she closes the door on him as I run to the bathroom and vomit for the third time tonight.

Mom knocks on my bedroom door. I don't answer. I heard her on the phone just now, talking to Dad, reiterating over and over that I was fine, that I'd rode around on the bus, that I was entitled to the way I was feeling, and to please just give me a bit of time. That sleeping on it would help pacify everyone's big feelings about whatever it was that happened tonight. I know he didn't hear a word she said. I didn't have to hear his end of the conversation to know that. He never hears things that don't fit the narrative he wants. I'm pretty sure I knew that before, deep down, but now I know it for real.

My door opens a crack. "He found your phone at the restaurant. He's insisting that he talk to you. He wants to hear from you, that you're okay."

"I couldn't care less what he wants right now."

"He says if he doesn't hear from you within thirty minutes, he's coming here to check on you himself." She hands me her phone. "Call, please."

My stomach cramps, and my palms get clammy. He hates coming here. He avoids it at all costs. And I know Mom doesn't want him showing up here. The neighbors are probably already wondering about us, having seen a cop at our door. We don't need any more drama tonight.

"You think he would?"

"He's pretty insistent."

I direct my gaze to my ceiling, fighting the burn of frustrated tears that threatens behind my eyes. Once again, he's designed it so that I don't have a choice.

"You know how persistent he can be when he wants something."

I know she's right, and I know he'll make this so much harder for both Mom and me if I don't do what he wants.

I call.

Mom steps out of my room. She pulls my door closed and a feeling of panic rises in me again.

Dad answers on the first ring. The words that blast through the phone at me are awful, but also exactly what I expected. When he's finished, I tell him I'm fine, but that I don't want to see him right now. And then I hang up.

A tear slips out, followed by another and another, and I slide my fingertips under my eyes, wiping them away. The door opens and Mom steps back in.

"Oh, Lexie." She sits next to me on the bed and hugs my shoulder, pulling me into her side. "You can talk to me. You can tell me anything."

I open my mouth, maybe to tell her that I'm fine, or maybe to tell her everything, but the ugly tears rush out. She holds me and I let my head fall on her shoulder, and we sit for a long time.

"I just … I don't understand," I say.

She rubs my arm. "Understand what?"

"It's like he doesn't see me. What I want makes no difference to him."

She rests her chin on the top of my head. "I'm sorry. I know how desperate you are for his approval."

I tell her then. I tell her things I've wanted to tell her for years but was always afraid to, for fear of what would happen if he found out I'd spilled his secrets. I tell her that I let him make her the villain. That he says she doesn't want us to be happy with him, and that it's her fault he has no money because the court lets her steal it all. I tell her that he hates when we talk about her, that he cuts her face out of all our family pictures, and that he thinks me wanting to go to Sunridge is her idea. Then I tell her the truth about why he's so short on money, and how he lets

Jonah skip school so he can go to work with him. And then I tell her about how I lied to her to get her to pay for Mav's vaccines.

She doesn't look surprised about any of it, and, not for the first time, I notice the dark circles under her eyes that she's tried to hide with foundation, and the deep creases in her forehead that showcase the weight of everything she's been trying to carry for me.

"You're not mad about the vaccines?"

"I'm only angry about the fact that you were put in a position where you felt you needed to do that. That you've had to carry that guilt around with you. I just …" She closes her eyes. "I don't know how to tell you how wrong it is that you've been forced to choose loyalties. You shouldn't have to choose between your father and me. I'm so sorry this has happened to you and Jonah. It's not your fault, Lexie. I don't blame you."

She grabs a tissue from my desk and hands it to me.

"You know I'm proud of you, right? And you should be proud of yourself for doing everything you've set out to do, even if your dad can't see it. I'm sorry he can't understand that you have your own goals and interests that are separate from his."

I look at her, wonder where the line is between not telling her certain things and being dishonest.

"You know he calls you the Controlling Bitch, right?"

She flinches.

"And Jonah believes everything he says. And he'll do anything he says, especially when Dad dangles the dirt bike carrot. It buys Jonah's loyalty every time. It's like he's Dad's puppet."

"I know," she says, her voice a quiet rasp. "I've been watching it happen."

Heat rises in me again, that she was aware of everything I'm telling her, but chose to say nothing. Do nothing.

"Why haven't you done anything to stop this?"

"What would you like me to do? Cut him out of our family photos? Should I call him names in front of you guys too? I refuse to play that game. All I can do is be the parent you and your brother need. The one that sets a decent example for you both. I hope that one day my efforts will pay off."

She looks away from me, tries to hide the tears pooling in the corners of her eyes, and the blame Dad layered on me turns to shame, that I swallowed his lies about her without question. I never dared question them, preferring to get comfortable with them, rather than risk being tossed aside for taking her side. My loyalty was always so reliable, but I see now how twisted it was.

"Don't tell your mother about the nice things I do for you, Lexie. She'll just get jealous, and twist things around, try to make me look bad."

"I need to ask you something," I say, even though I think I know the answer. Dad would say it so often though, that it became truth, and I stopped questioning the reality of it. Trying to correct it meant I was taking her side.

"Of course."

"Do you take meds?"

Her grip on my knee stiffens and her mouth freezes into a thin line. "No, I don't. Nor have I ever."

"You won't tell him what I told you, will you?"

He can't know, because then he'll toss me aside for real. I tell myself it will be better that way, but I'm not sure it would be, and I hate that I care so much.

She shakes her head. "No. The secrets he makes you keep are safe with me. I understand your fear."

The next few days blurred together. I felt cut off from my friends. I'd reach for my phone, but then remember all over again that Dad had it. I wasn't about to go over there and get it because then he would win: I'd have to see him in person and he'd hook me back in. It was a strange emptiness, not hearing from Dad.

I stayed up half the night, writing down everything that happened at Weezie's and before in my journal, so I wouldn't forget, because my mind's been spinning around and around with how Dad says what happened compared to how I know it really happened, and I'm having trouble separating one event from the other. I wrote and wrote until my hand cramped up, and then wrote some more. After I got it all down, I saw how much I'd been carrying, and my thoughts felt less tangled. And now I have a record of it I can refer to when Dad tells me I'm remembering things wrong. The truth in my own handwriting doesn't lie like he does.

I feel bad for Mom though, because now she has to deal with the mess I made. She hasn't said so, but I don't need to be a genius to figure out who keeps calling and texting her. She was in the kitchen washing the dishes when he called her again last night. I heard their conversation through the duct in my room, when I accidentally-on-purpose fell into my closet and my ear landed on it. She doesn't know that I can hear everything she says in the kitchen through the vent in my room. Almost every night after dinner, she puts her phone on speaker and talks to either my aunt or Grandma while she washes the dishes. Most of the time her conversations don't interest me, but when I heard her talking in a more agitated tone with no speaker, I had to know what was going on.

"No, I have never told Lexie not to go there," Mom said. "You're wrong, I'm not keeping her from you. Whatever happened between you two has nothing to do with me. Give her some space. I think she feels that you don't understand her ... What has Jonah got to do with —"

That was all I heard. Mom turned the water back on and that was the end of my eavesdropping.

CHAPTER TWENTY-THREE

TUESDAY, MARCH 19

It's hard to believe, but his place looks worse than I remember, even though it's only been five days since I was last here. I don't know how I never noticed the level of unkemptness before, and embarrassment floods through me, that Nate is with me, seeing it in its full not-glory. The bush under the front window that's been in dire need of a weed whacker for some time competes with a maple tree that's invaded its center, and it looks as if the two plants are locked in battle to see who can swallow up the entirety of the front window first. Our dented metal garbage can, struggling but failing to contain its rank contents, is wedged between the cracked concrete of the front porch and the pile of broken cinder blocks that Dad needed for some project that he never started. The screen door hangs open, bumps against the garbage bin, and the mailbox clings lopsided to the faded milky coffee-colored clapboard that wraps the house.

"So which house is it?" Nate asks, turning into the alley behind it.

I asked him to help me. I had to get Mav out. It should've

been Zara who helped me, but she's still determined to be mad at me for leaving the party with Rhys. I'm relieved Nate didn't ask too many questions about why I wanted to steal my own dog, because that'd be the first question I would've asked. I'm also relieved that we're also both pretending that our quasi-argument last week about Rhys never happened. I wish Zara would do the same.

"That one," I say, pointing across the alley. "The one with the porch light on."

All the houses look the same, with their tiny backyards. It used to have a proper lawn that mom would mow every week, with a sandbox at the back and a small vegetable garden along the side where she grew tomatoes and strawberries. Dad tore it all up after she left. He wanted to build a fishpond, like the one he saw on YouTube. He and Jonah got as far as digging the hole for it. Now, almost four years later, the yard's still a heaved mess covered in weeds. Our old wagon, which Mom used to pull Jonah and me to the playground in, is now a sickly pink color from too many days left in the sun, still filled with dirt from the excavation, its wheels sunken into the earth.

Nate parks well away from the lights that bathe the street from overhead.

"You sure you want to do this?"

His eyes have a look in them, like he feels sorry for me, and it makes the canyon-sized conflict of interest that's taking up every square inch of my thoughts scream at me, because there's nothing worse than pity when you're guilty of something. I shove the guilt off though, because there's been nothing to suggest anything's wrong with the work Dad's been doing at the OldMill, and as much as I hope his business fails, I also hope this backward arrangement works out because if it doesn't, he won't be able to pay his rent, which will be my fault, as Dad's made crystal clear. My guilt sidles back on my shoulders.

"I'm sure," I say, ignoring the fact that my gut's turned into mush, determined to proceed with the plan. "Mav can't stay here if I'm not here. I'll never forgive myself if I don't find a better place for him."

He nods, but I see the questions he's not asking behind his eyes. "I'll meet you behind the automotive garage like we planned. You sure they're not home?"

I nod. Jonah had said something about having to go out of town to Dad's friend's place to pick up some sort of saw they needed to do a job. My guilt-o-meter raged even higher when I heard that. No doubt the job was Nate's.

I slide myself out of his truck. We've been over the plan a few times: go in, leash Mav with the leash I brought, and leave, "forgetting" to latch the door. Then, use the shadows of the alleyway to make it back to Nate's car. Easy peasy.

I close the truck door and focus my eyes into the shadows that stretch toward the rear of Dad's yard, trying to reassure myself that no one's watching. Tonight, I welcome the cover they'll provide, whereas on any other night, I've feared what they hid, just out of my reach.

My heart thunders in my ears as I pick my way along the edge of the alleyway. I'm within a few steps of our yard when Mrs. Jones, our next-door neighbor, flicks her porch light on and throws open her back door, her arms full of empty bottles destined for her recycle bins. I jump back and hide against the wall of her backyard shed, while my heart bounces around like a herd of thundering elephants. It's a wonder she can't hear it. Of all the neighbors to avoid, she's number one, but it's not because I don't like her. In fact, it's the opposite. She'll want to strike up a conversation, which will blow my cover. I can't risk it.

A whispery clicking sound comes from behind me, and a stiff tail licks my pant leg. A rat! Scrambling, I knock into a tower of old paint cans stacked behind the shed. The clatter of the falling cans sends the rat squealing and sets Mav barking from inside the house. *CRAP!*

"Who's there?" Mrs. Jones calls out, her voice wavering. "You get out of here, you hear me? I'll call the police!"

I flatten myself against the wall of the shed and try not to breathe. The only thing keeping me from absolute panic is knowing that she's not going to come down and look for herself. I know she's too scared. Seconds tick by, each one feeling like nine hundred. Aside from Mav's barking, the night is quiet again. Mrs. Jones's feet make shuffling sounds on her porch, and I don't have to see her to know she's scanning the alleyway, squinting into the shadows.

"Damned racoons," she mumbles. The door creaks open and then clicks shut behind her, but her light stays on, its glare swallowing the shadows I was planning to skirt through.

I count to ten and make a run for it. I stay low to the ground, sneak along the back of Mrs. Jones's yard until I reach the rear of Dad's and climb the three crooked cement steps to the door. The noise of my key jabbing into the lock sends an already excited Mav into a frenzy. I crack the door open and squeeze myself inside. I don't dare open it too far. All I need to screw this up is for Mav to run out before I can get his leash on. I smell his neglect instantly, and any guilt I have about what I'm about to do disappears. I'm shocked by it, but I'm also not. It's happened before, when we were at Mom's for a couple days, when Dad promised to take care of him and then didn't. A quick glance at his bowls — one empty, the other with hardly a slosh of water — does nothing but reinforce my resolve. Mav's all over me though, his paws on my shoulders, tail swishing back and forth 180 degrees. He yips with excitement as his wet nose nuzzles my ear and neck, giving me his best version of a hug a dog can give. Tears prickle behind my eyes and I stifle a sob, burying my face in his neck. I know it's the best thing for him. And for me.

"Easy boy," I say, pushing him down so all his feet are on the floor. He leans into my knees, letting me rub him behind his ears. "I missed you too. Do you want to go for a walk?"

He sits, his eyes bright, focused on me. I bend down and clip the leash to his collar.

I see the usual jumble of unopened bills on the floor by the side of the door. The corner of my phone peeks out from under them. Am I surprised that my phone is treated like trash by Dad? Not really. I grab it and stick it in my pocket and walk Mav out into the night for the last time. My tears flow like a river running over its banks, but I don't bother wiping them away.

CHAPTER TWENTY-FOUR

TUESDAY, MARCH 26

I pick at the loose thread on the arm of the loveseat. Someone else must've been picking at it since I sat here last, because it's been further sprung from its stitching. Dr. Crowchild retrieves two bottles of Perrier from the small fridge next to her window, and I can't help but notice the new plant in the center, its leaves fanning out wide, seeming to hold the weight of its abundant purple flowers. I find it annoying that Dr. Crowchild's plants always look so bright and healthy, while the one I've been trying to keep alive seems to fight against my efforts willing it to thrive. Despite the fact that I've been watering Mr. Harris's plant, and rotating its position in the window, it still looks like a barren stick. I even shoved some plant fertilizer sticks that I found buried in Mom's shed into the soil, and still nothing.

"Oh give up already! How many times do I have to tell you? You can't love life back into it."

She twists the caps off both bottles and puts one on the table in front of me.

"It's nice to see you again. I was happy to hear that it was you that called this morning, wanting to see me, and not your mom. What brings you in today?"

I grab the cold bottle and take a sip, letting the fizz burn on my tongue. I've rehearsed how this conversation would go a few times, but now I'm second-guessing myself again. It's another thing I have to work on. I can never just be satisfied with a decision I make. I always question whether or not it's the right one, an eternal loop that won't shut up. Closing my eyes, I take a deep breath and count to ten, trying to get a handle on what I came here to ask her. She says nothing and waits patiently. I don't want to talk about it and betray him, but also because if I do talk about it, it'll make his real self be even more real, and I'm not sure I'm ready to deal with the entirety of that.

"I took your advice about making my priorities priorities again, and told my dad what my plans were. It didn't go very well."

"How do you feel about that?"

"I don't know. I feel a lot of things. I'm not sure what's right and what's wrong."

Her voice is quiet, patient. She leans forward and touches my knee. "There are no right or wrong feelings, Lexie. You're entitled to them all. You do understand that, don't you?"

I nod, even though I don't. Not really.

"You shouldn't feel that way, Lexie. You're overreacting again. We'd get along a lot better if you'd just learn to chill out."

"Do you want to tell me what happened?"

The sympathy that exudes from her voice gives me the permission I've been looking for to talk to her, to get her advice, because I still can't be sure that it's not me that's the problem.

My eyes flicker to the clock on her desk.

"Don't worry about the time. I've got nowhere else to be."

I shake my head. "So much has happened. I don't even know where to start."

"Why don't you start by telling me what happened when you tried to tell him what you needed to tell him."

My eyes meet hers then, and I see a realness in them, a genuine concern for me. It makes me feel like maybe I am justified in seeking her opinion, and I decide I can trust her to help me figure out what's real and what's not, and I repeat it all again. I talk and talk and talk. It's like she pulled the end of a ball of yarn and it spills out on the table between us, a big, unorganized mess with no end or beginning. She interrupts me a lot, sometimes asking me to repeat something I said, and sometimes it's with another question aimed at clarifying how and why certain things happened. She fills page after page of her yellow lined legal pad. Sometime while I'm talking, she puts another bottle of Perrier in front of me. When I stop talking, the streetlights are on outside.

"Thank you for trusting me with all of that. I can see what a burden it's been for you."

She sits back in her chair, crosses her legs.

"Your ability to self-reflect is impressive. I've never met anyone as young as you who is so desperate to find and correct their own faults, but I have to tell you, I don't see that you've done anything wrong. None of what happened is your fault."

"It's not your fault, Lexie. I don't blame you."

There's a long pause as her words sink in, and I try to sort out what she's telling me into something that's true.

"But that doesn't make any sense," I say. "It takes two people to have a disagreement. I see now that it's not all me, but some of it has to be my fault. Doesn't it?"

A slight tension flexes through her jaw, and a sharpness appears in her eyes that I've not seen before. She hesitates before she speaks, like she's sifting through words, making sure she chooses the right ones. "In a normal, healthy relationship I would agree with you, but I don't believe that's the case here."

"I don't understand."

She leans forward in her chair, her elbows on her knees. "When you talk to your dad, do you feel that you can trust him to listen to you and accept you, and that there's a shared feeling of give and take?"

Her question lands at my feet with a thud. Like the soccer ball that Mav sunk his teeth into.

She continues. "In healthy relationships, both parties want the same things. And by things, I mean things like love, trust, and mutual respect. The reason you're having difficulty communicating with your dad is because your relationship with him isn't like that, but rather, it's all based on what he wants. Him not wanting you to go to the school of your choice is about him, the family business is about what he wants, and now his demands to see you on his terms is about him and what he feels he's entitled to. There is no give and take, only him taking. And all you've been doing is giving. The issue between the two of you has nothing to do with him being overprotective, as you said. That's just the excuse he uses to get away with what's happening. I think his default of 'I'm your father so I know best' has nothing to do with your best interests and everything to do with his control over you."

It's like she poured a bucket of ice water over my head. I want to tell her that she's got it wrong, that it's not like that, but I'm not sure it's true.

"And so now I have to ask you if you still believe that your relationship with him used to be 'easier' and 'simpler.' Is that the case? Or were you younger then, and happy to spend time doing whatever your dad wanted to do? And by always being the girl he trained you to be, he was very happy with you, wasn't he?"

Her voice is echoey, like she's in a tunnel. My brain is busy trying to rearrange what she's turned inside out.

"The thing that's different now is that you're trying to be the person you want to be, rather than the one he wants you to be, to serve his needs. Would you say that's accurate?"

I feel numb. I think about all the times I blindly followed him around, doing his bidding, happy that there was a place for me in his world. Then I think about all the times he showed up for me. Exactly zero. He didn't even show up at the hospital, after an awful weekend at his house landed me there with a panic attack, the reason I ended up here, in this chair. Mom always showed up though. Shame washes over me again that I ever allowed him to make me doubt her.

She leans back in her chair, switches her legs. "Your father's conditioned you to feel selfish for wanting to do anything other than serve his needs, so that you feel guilty for wanting to become the person you want to be for yourself, and while I applaud you for trying to find and correct your faults, it's your need to do so that he exploits. It's to his advantage to have you believing that this is your fault. To have you believe the lies he's programmed you to believe about yourself."

"You mean that I'm selfish?"

"Exactly. You also said you feel confused. That's the way he wants you. Keeping you mentally trapped, wondering what you did to deserve to be treated so poorly, is what keeps you under his control, always looking for the tiniest sliver of approval."

Silent tears course down my cheeks. I understand what she's saying is mostly true, but I have to believe that he's not always like she says, because he can be good to me too. Once he apologizes and decides to listen to me, things can get better again.

She hands me a tissue and I wipe my eyes. "Sorry."

"For what?"

"I didn't think I'd cry."

"There's nothing wrong with crying, Lexie."

She waits for a moment while I sip at my Perrier.

"So how do I make this better?"

She gives me a sad smile. "You'd better call your mom and tell her we're going to be a while longer. I need to teach you a few things about boundaries."

CHAPTER TWENTY-FIVE

FRIDAY, APRIL 5

The sun's barely kissed the ground when I walk through the doors of the recreation center. The humid, chlorine-tainted air warms me, and is a welcome reminder of the solitude I've been pining for. I do my best to let go of the elusive dusting of guilt that threatens the peace I've made with myself. A wisp of it floats through my thoughts like a string of sticky spider webbing, always clinging to me somewhere, refusing to let go entirely.

I left a message for Rhys that I was going to the pool. I didn't want him to hear from someone else that I'd come and not told him, but I'm hoping he doesn't show up. It's not that I don't want to swim with him. It's just that I miss the peace and quiet of just me. It's been so long since I've had it. There's also the fact that I know my practice is much better when he's not with me, and good practice is what I need right now. The spring meet is coming up, and I can't afford to not get that scholarship. I'll never let him know though, that I'm faster than him. He has no idea that when we swim together, I ease up on the clock. I could tell he didn't like it the one time that I did swim a better time than him, and I didn't bother arguing with him when he insisted that he let me win. I didn't want to be that kind of girlfriend.

I push against the change room door but my shoulder bounces off it. It's then that I remember the email that said we'd need our key fobs to access the pool if we wanted to swim before eight a.m. on weekdays.

Crouching on the floor in front of the door with my swim bag at my feet, I unzip my bag and run my hands in and out of every pocket multiple times, looking for my fob. A frustrated heat rises in me when I can't find it. I know where it is. In the little dish I keep on my desk that holds stuff I like to keep handy like paper clips, bobby pins, and my favorite passion fruit–watermelon lip moisturizer. I put it there so it wouldn't get lost when I was cleaning out my bag two days ago. I press my forehead to the door, a groan escaping my lips. This is not the practice I was hoping for.

"Forget your fob?"

My heart stumbles over itself. Zara's standing behind me, her normally perfect hair piled on top of her head in a loose knot, small tendrils frizzing out along her hairline.

"Jeez, you scared me. What are you doing here?"

It's a valid question, because Zara doesn't get up early. It's not something she's capable of. Not to mention that she's wearing sweatpants that have seen too many wears, and a way-too-big T-shirt that says "I need vitamin sea" that I'm pretty sure is her dad's.

"I saw you walk by," she says. "I thought maybe we could talk, or that we need to talk, or um, that I need to talk to you."

Her eyes look dark and glassy, like she's pulled too many all-nighters.

"Okay," I say, now a bit worried, but also wondering what the urgency is when she could have responded to any one of the bazillion texts I sent her in the last month, or even the one I sent last night.

She sucks a sharp breath over her teeth. "Today my dad and I have to —"

Just at that moment, my phone explodes with "It's your boyfriend calling! It's your boyfriend calling!"

Zara pulls a face, and I instantly regret the stupid, obnoxious ringtone I picked, which for some reason is set to maximum volume.

"Sorry," I say, as I fumble around in the depths of my bag, missing it multiple times in my desperation to turn it off while it keeps screaming its obnoxious announcement. Finally, my fingers find it and flick it to mute.

"You could've answered it," she says, but the way she says it makes me glad I didn't.

"It's okay." I steady my gaze on her. "You and your dad have to do what?"

She starts again, just as I see a text from Rhys flash across the screen. I glance at it, try to see what he wants while she's talking, but then I realize she's stopped.

"Are you even going to pretend to listen to me?"

Her accusation jabs me, like the pointed end of a stick.

"Zara, I'm not the one who's been ignoring all the messages you haven't sent me."

Her face softens, and she looks almost ashamed. "You're right. I'm sorry. It's been a lot. I'm just —"

She presses her hands together and squeezes her eyes shut, like she's gathering a whole bunch of things. I relax, feel sorry for sniping at her. She starts talking again, but another message flashes across my screen. I try not to look, but I can't not look.

I'll pick you up.

Wait. What? No. No, no, no. I don't need a ride. I'm already here. Jeez. I have to tell him.

"— wondering if you wanted to help me with it." Her voice jerks me back.

"Help with what?" I ask, picking up my phone.

"Did you hear anything I said?"

Her voice is suddenly all shouty, and I'm annoyed that after weeks of nothing, now she needs all of me, all at once.

"She's selfish, Lexie. Don't you see that?"

I resist the urge to scream at her to just spit it out, to just tell me what she needs to tell me.

"Yes, I heard you," I lie. "Just give me two seconds."

I turn away from her to text Rhys.

"I don't have a lot of time, Lexie."

When I turn back around, she's gone

CHAPTER TWENTY-SIX

FRIDAY, APRIL 12

My neglect of the office is obvious. The stack of mail and paperwork in the "IN" tray is again much higher than the stack in the "OUT" tray. I sigh. At least it isn't still sitting in the mailbox outside.

For once I'm glad that Nate isn't here. I wasn't planning on coming today, but when I saw that his truck was gone, I came here instead of going home after I was finished at the pool. It's not that I don't want to see him, it's just that it'll be faster to get through the paperwork if I have the place to myself.

Dropping my bag on the floor beside the desk, I slide into the roller chair and start the process of opening the mail and sorting it into piles. Invoices for money owed, receipts for purchases made, junk mail, quotes for repairs to the roof and the sink that's leaking in the bathroom. I cringe seeing that, once again, the stack of bills exceeds the height of the other piles. I file the receipts away and sort the quotations from least expensive to most, and turn to the stack of bills. Thankfully there are only three this time.

Once the mail's sorted, I turn on the computer to check the marina's email and notice another envelope that I missed, wedged behind the monitor. Sliding my thumb under the sealed edge, I rip it open and recognize Dad's clumsy handwriting. I drop it like it's fire, watch it flutter to the floor while I count and breathe, count and breathe, forcing my hammering heart to chill out. I remind myself that there's nothing wrong with paperwork coming to this office from Dad. That it's to be expected, given that he's their contractor. That it doesn't mean anything's wrong.

Feeling ridiculous, I retrieve the receipt from the floor and a brick falls through my stomach. It's for a skid of porcelain subway tile, for over nineteen hundred dollars. Stamped in the middle of the page is "PAID. Thank you." Along the bottom is a note:

Additional tile needed for bathrooms.

The receipt trembles in my hand, and I blink, but I know that no amount of blinking will make it right. I know what tile this is, and I know it didn't go into the bathrooms at the OldMill.

"Lexie, I need you to sell this tile for me on one of those buy and sell groups."

"Sure, Dad. How much do you want for it?"

"Just put $1600.00 OBO."

Oh no. No, no, no, no, no.

A roaring fills my ears and the walls around me start turning, folding in on themselves. I hold my stomach, will the squall that's started raging to calm down. I lean forward and rest my forehead on the edge of the desk and breathe. In, two, three, four; out, two, three, four. I can't believe he did this. Except that I can. It's what I was worried about, what I hoped wouldn't happen, and I let it happen anyway. I could've stopped it, prevented Dad from doing what I knew he'd do, but I didn't. I let my self-serving need to help Dad get what he wanted, so that I could have what I wanted, get in the way of protecting Nate, and what he wants, and what Pops wanted for the marina.

"I couldn't have done this without you, Lexie. You know that, right?"

I'm a horrible person. A terrible friend. How do I fix this? How could I have been so stupid to think —

The door at the back of the garage bangs shut. "Lexie? You here?" It's Nate.

"Yeah," my voice shakes out. "I'm in the office."

My butterflies are carrying rocks. No. Not rocks. Giant boulders, dragging them up my throat. I have to tell him. I can't not tell him anymore. I can't let Dad get away with this.

"I didn't know you were — whoa." He stops in the doorway, concern written over every inch of his face. "Are you okay?"

I rake a breath over my teeth, try to take back some air. "I need to tell you something."

His forehead creases. "You're freaking me out a bit. Should I be worried?"

I hand him the receipt. He looks at it and lifts a shoulder. "I don't get it."

"The materials listed on that receipt, that you paid for, weren't used for the job," I say.

Confusion works its way across his face. "Even if that is true, how would you know that?"

My palms are slick, and I think I might throw up.

"Because your contractor is my dad, and he made me sell that tile, and —"

What I need to tell him nearly crowds the air from my lungs, but I push through. I need to tell him all of it. I can't not tell him all of it.

"— and he's not a licensed plumber. He's not a licensed or insured anything. He's a fraud. The license he gave you is fake. I know, because I made it for him."

He flinches, tries to hide the pocket-sized earthquake that shakes down his spine. He looks like he's thinking hard to make sense of something that doesn't make sense.

"I didn't know that he invoiced you for that tile until now. I didn't think that was something he'd do."

Lie.

Disappointment rolls off him in waves. His gaze, like frost, lands on mine. "But you knew he was working for us and that he was a fraud, and you never said anything."

I divert my eyes from his. I can't bear the accusatory look on his face. I try to explain my reasoning. I tell him the rest of what I should have told him the night we took Mav, but that it should've been okay because, despite his fake license, Dad's capable of doing the job he was hired to do. But then I hear myself defending him, justifying his lawbreaking, parroting his words, hear my excuses for him dissolve into nothing worthwhile, and my shame rolls back in like a relentless echo, its heaviness spreading out like wet concrete on my shoulders. Deep down, when I hear myself say the real truth out loud, I know it sounds ridiculous, even though I also know it isn't. Not really.

"I'm sorry," I say.

He says nothing, looks at me like he's seeing something he's never seen before, and that's when I know how royally I've screwed things up, because being looked at like you're nothing, like you don't even exist, is worse than anything. I wish I could say I don't know that, but I do. It's a feeling I'm familiar with even though I often try to convince myself that my feelings about that aren't real.

He steps away from me, his palms raised. "I can't be here with you. Lock up when you leave. I can't believe that you, of all people —" His voice breaks off, and he turns away.

"Wait! Nate!" I stifle a sob that's fighting to burst my chest into a million pieces.

He stops. His body is rigid, hands clamped tight at his sides.

"Get an inspector in there. It's probably fine, but —" I stop myself, because there I go again. Defending him. I hate myself.

He doesn't answer. Or if he does, I don't hear it over the slam of the door.

CHAPTER TWENTY-SEVEN

MID- TO LATE APRIL

The days drip by. The snow melts, the trees bud, and tulips start to push their way free of the hard-packed soil. I manage the essentials: school, swim, homework. I start another Moleskine sketchbook, this one for pastels and watercolors. I manage to beat my personal best in the pool. Mom's birthday comes and goes with no sign of Jonah. She thinks I don't notice, but I see her wiping her eyes. The cherry blossom season peaks in Washington, and I'd give just about anything to go there and just sketch and paint and hide. Instead, I bake more banana chocolate chip muffins than Mom and I can eat, and I watch *This Is Us* on repeat. Dad's barrage of texts started within a day of me having my phone back, but he doesn't mention Mav, not even once.

His calling and texting makes my palms sweat and my insides tumble into each other. I keep ignoring, and Jonah texts, demanding that I stop behaving like a spoiled child and have a real conversation. I tell him Dad can tell me that himself, that he doesn't have to be his messenger. Mom and I both try hard to pretend that things are normal, that nothing's wrong, like we're swimming in a tranquil lake, the sunlight rolling over the gentle ripples in the water, rather than fighting to stay afloat in a tumultuous ocean, while its massive waves crash over us, steal our breath, pull us under.

It rains for days and days. I clean the house, reorganize the linen closet, teach myself how to fold fitted sheets. The days go on and on, daylight, moonlight, daylight again. I feel like there's a part of me that's hollow, like I'm dried up, like Mr. Harris's plant that just continues to refuse all of my efforts to make it whole again. Like a lake devoid of water.

Spring pokes its head out and then disappears again, and I spend hours wondering how I got here. How everything I've done over the last bit of forever to keep everyone happy has blown up in my face. Neither Nate or Zara will respond to my calls or texts, Jonah won't talk to Mom, and the one person I want some distance from won't leave me alone. I think that's called irony. His accusations ring in my ears, and it hurts all over again, like he kicked me in the stomach. I think about blocking his number, but part of me wants to see that he's trying, even if it's to blame me for everything he did. It means maybe he still does love me, even if just a little, because he wouldn't try if he didn't, right? Jonah texts to tell me that he'll talk to Mom again when I stop being mean to Dad, and my guilt weighs on me, drags me down like an anchor, leaving me gasping for forgiveness, that Jonah and Mom are being punished for what I refuse to do. I sleep in his bed, hoping the weight of his blankets negates some of the weight of his absence, and I spend hours and hours trying to figure out a way to fix things without giving up all the pieces of myself I've worked so hard for.

A package comes from Dad and my breath goes solid. When I open it, memories wash over me. It's a tin of Simpkins travel sweets, tropical fruit mix (the best mix), and a pink Moleskine sketchbook. Dad always used to keep a tin of the candy in the console of his car, and I'd always sneak outside and pick out the pineapple ones. He'd pretend to get mad that I ate his candy again, and I'd giggle and deny it, my tongue raw and tingly from too much sugar. In reality, we both knew that he bought them for me. Mom and Jonah never knew our secret. It was a special thing, between just us. I open the sketchbook. A note falls from between its pages.

I'm sorry you misinterpreted things. I'm only trying to do what's best for you, but you're not making it easy. Let's put this behind us and start over. I forgive you and love you.

I slam it shut, file it in my garbage can. I don't think I like pink, even though Dad always told me it was my favorite color. I hide in the dark under my comforter with my travel sweets, furious, but mostly weary of it all. I suck on two at once, just like I used to, but the candy is sharp and cuts my tongue.

Another weekend comes and goes without me going to the marina and Mom wants to know why. I tell her that there are some repairs ongoing there, and I don't want to get in the way, and then I change the subject and ask her about her book club. I tell myself that it's not lying since it is, partly, sort of true. I go out with Rhys, even though I don't have the energy to pretend I want to. He doesn't seem to notice and I let him love me the way he wants to, so that he doesn't leave me too. I tell myself it was fine, that I had a good time, that in the end it was good to get out and forget that my dad, my brother, and my friends all hate me, but I'm not sure that I mean it.

I forget my phone when Mom drags me out of the house to go for a hike along the gorge. At the edge of a clearing we see a deer grazing on the long grasses. I look for her baby, but don't see it. A hawk circles above, riding on the thermals, searching for mice tunneling through the fields. We follow the stream and pass two waterfalls, one above our heads, spilling from the top of the gorge, the other tiny, tumbling over the rocks that crowd it where it narrows. We take selfies together; both of us smile big, like if we smile big enough, it'll wipe away all the bad, even if it's only for a few blissful hours. After, we stop for coffee and donuts. I get a chocolate glazed and Mom gets a Boston cream. It's a good day. When we need to put our jackets on, we go home, back to pretending that we're fine, just fine. I check my phone and find two messages from Dad and my stomach turns its usual cartwheel.

You could at least say thank you.
Ignoring people is infantile behavior. Did you know that?

I type out a response. I want to remind him of where I learned it from. But I delete it and turn off my phone. I know that nothing I say will matter anyway. I can't make him understand, when he's committed to not understanding me at all.

The weather warms enough to open the windows, then it gets frigid again, and then it rains buckets and everything turns to ice. I practice sketching waterfalls. He texts, telling me he doesn't want to see me. That until I do what's right and "drop this silly art school bit," he doesn't want to see or talk to me. I tell myself I'm grateful for the peace, but I'm not sure I believe it. I suck on another travel sweet, this one guava flavor, and a memory sneaks up on me before I can stop it. We were on the couch, watching a movie. Jonah was curled up against Mom, her arm around him. I curled myself into Dad, hoping for the same. He huffed out a sigh and moved away from me, to the armchair. I pretended I was happy for the space so he didn't feel bad. I'd taken a guava travel sweet from his tin of candy earlier that day, rather than my usual pineapple. Maybe that was why he was mad. I file the tin of candy in my garbage can, next to the sketchbook.

Dad keeps trying, keeps texting. It seems he can't follow through on his threat to not speak to me until I do what he demands.

Are you still mad? Ask your mother what she takes to deal with her rage issues. Maybe it'll help you get along with me better.

Then:

When are you going to get over this?

I consult the list of reminders about boundaries Dr. Crowchild had me write in my journal: It's okay to say no, it's okay if people don't agree with me, it's okay to be myself and not what others want me to be, it's not my job to take care of other people's needs; the people who get upset about my boundaries are the ones who benefit from me not having any. Then I seal up the cracks between my boundaries and feel like I've won. That is until he texts again:

We finished the job at the OldMill. I need you to help us find another contract.

His lie is glaring, and I know, without actually knowing, that they fired him.

Please Lexie. You'd do it if you cared.
It'll be your fault when we can't pay the rent.

My guilt tries to slink back in, but I refuse to wear it, and I can't help feeling the tiniest bit relieved to know that he still needs me. Then I feel the cracks between my boundaries start to open, and I hate myself all over again.

CHAPTER TWENTY-EIGHT

FRIDAY, MAY 3

School lets out early because of a rugby game. I was hoping to go to the pool for an hour of extra practice, especially now that the meet is only six weeks away, but it's closed for maintenance. I could go to the office, since I know there's another pile of stuff waiting for me, but Nate still hasn't responded to any of my messages. If he's there, I know I won't be able to handle it if he looks at me the way he looked at me that night. I could just go home, but Mom won't be home yet, and despite the digital media assignment that I have to work on, my mind's not where it needs to be to make any real progress on it.

I decide to pay a surprise visit to Mr. Harris. It's been way too long since I've seen him. I'm sure he'll have a snide comment about me not knowing the days of the week, but I know he'll be pleased to see me, even if he won't come out and say it.

I get there earlier than I normally would, so after I sign in, I go straight to the activity room. I know he often goes there to watch *Jeopardy!* and play cribbage with some of the other residents in the afternoons. At least he always used to. It seems that the last few times I saw him, he got tired quickly, so he's not always up for it. He's not there though, so I loop around the back hallway to his room, in the far back corner of the residence. It's in the new wing of the building, which finished construction last summer. His room used to be closer to the lobby, but he complained everyday, to anyone within earshot, that that room was too noisy and too close to all the senile old people who talked too much. They moved him as soon as they could. I'm pretty sure he drove them crazy.

As I round the corner, the redolent odor of fresh paint replaces the heavy stale smell that permeates the rest of the building, and I curse when I see that, once again, Mr. Harris's plant is in the hallway outside his door.

How many times were we going to have this argument?

I tuck the pot under my arm, try not to be irritated that it still looks awful and maybe even worse than last time.

"Mr. Harris?" I call into his room from the doorway. "It's Lexie. I rescued your plant again. Are you up for a game of Scrabble today?"

There's no response, so I step farther into the room, only to find an empty space with freshly painted white walls. A box is on the floor pushed up against the wall, filled with the contents of what was on Mr. Harris's nightstand: his dictionary and Scrabble board, a copy of *Moby Dick*, and the two framed photos he kept: one of him and his husband, the other of a woman with a young girl.

"Hey." A guy wearing paint-splattered clothes appears behind me, a cup of Starbucks in his hand. "This room's off limits."

"Did Mr. Harris change rooms again?"

"No idea. You'll have to ask —"

"Lexie. It is you." Valerie Blakeman, the wife of Dad's previous boss, and the volunteer and activities coordinator here. She leans on the doorjamb, breathless. "I wasn't expecting you today."

"School let out early so I came to see Mr. Harris," I say.

Her lips turn up in a forced smile and her eyes settle, heavy on mine. That's when the tone between us changes, and the reality of the empty room dawns on me. My stomach drops like an anchor, into the floor.

"No," I hear myself croak out.

"I'm sorry, hon."

The floor tilts sideways, and I grab the wall with my free hand to steady myself. Valerie reaches for my elbow and says something, but I can't hear her over the throbbing that fills my ears. The paint fumes take hold of my throat, choking me, and the room suddenly feels about 50 degrees hotter than it should. I feel disconnected, somehow outside of myself and far away, like I'm watching myself from above.

"I think maybe you should sit for a minute," I hear her say, feel her guide me by my elbow.

I pull myself free of her grasp and press my feet to move forward, one in front of the other, out of his room, back down the hall, to the lobby, to outside. I hear her calling after me, but I don't turn around. I can't. I just need to get out.

My vision blurry, I find my way outside to the terrace and sit at the table Mr. Harris and I used to sit at, back when he was feeling well enough to go outside. I give his plant a shake, and a few more dry leaves fall off. I hear him tell me, like he's right beside me, to stop wasting my time on "that ugly stump of a plant." Tears drip from my chin, soaking the front of my shirt, but I don't care. I sit, watching but not watching life go on around me, wondering how it's possible when someone so important just died. Visitors and staff come and go. A car runs a red light, almost causing an accident. Carpenter bees buzz in and out of a hole in the garden pergola. A driver delivers food to a house across the street. A mama robin hops after her fledgling, her offering of food dangling from her beak.

My phone buzzes from somewhere in the depths of my backpack but I don't have the energy to answer it, and I hardly notice when the sun slips beneath the treetops and the sky changes from blue to violet to indigo. As night presses on, a car door slams somewhere nearby. Footsteps approach, get louder.

"Lexie."

A voice behind me. Concerned. Nate's voice.

"I've been looking all over for you. Your mom's worried."

I don't look at him. I can't. I feel his eyes bore into me, like he's trying to read my thoughts. I'm glad he's here, but I can't tell him that. He unzips his hoodie and places it around me before he slides in next to me, his thigh warm against mine. It's only then that I notice I'm shivering. His arm wraps over my shoulder, coaxing me to lean into the solid comfort of his chest. I let him pull me in, and it feels good and right, like we somehow fit together, like the moon and the stars. He says nothing. He doesn't have to. I give in to all my feelings then, and let my head fall against his shoulder. Piles and piles of regret, guilt, and grief spill over, a torrent I can't stop. He holds me while my shoulders shake and the sun relinquishes its last beam, giving way to blackness.

CHAPTER TWENTY-NINE

FRIDAY, MAY 3

We sat there for a while, under the light of the moon, while I went to pieces. I remember telling him between sobs that Mr. Harris had died, and him hugging me tighter, telling me that he was sorry. I guess he got me in his truck at some point because now I'm sitting on Gertrude with a crocheted blanket tucked around me, and a cup of hot chocolate in my hands. It has tiny marshmallows in it. They don't taste like anything, but they make it seem more authentic somehow. He's sitting next to me, his hands inches from mine, and I want him to pull me into him again. It felt safe there, relaxed, and I want to feel that again, and I can't help wondering why I've not felt that way when Rhys holds me.

"Are you okay?" he asks, his voice soft. His milky brown eyes, flecked with green, peer at me from behind his thick lashes.

I fight a fresh wave of tears. "I don't know. I'm better now that at least you're speaking to me again."

Guilt shines in his eyes. "I'm sorry. When you told me about your dad, and all of what he did and was doing, I was shocked, and then angry, and then hurt, that" — he pauses like he's trying to decide how much he should say — "well, that it came from you."

I look away, as my own guilt slides back into its place on my shoulders like it thinks it belongs there.

"I shouldn't have reacted the way I did, especially since I was fairly certain it wasn't your fault."

Wasn't my fault. There's that lie again. Everyone keeps saying that.

"But it was my fault. I could've stopped it. Stopped him. I chose not to."

To get what I wanted.

"But if you did stop it," he says, "what would've been the consequence?"

His question slams into me, like a truck with no brakes, reminds me of what I now know. Makes sure I don't forget.

Please Lexie. I need you. You'd do it if you cared.
It'll be your fault if the business falls apart.
How could you do this to me, your own dad?

"The thing that happened with your dog, that's when things finally clicked for me."

My brow hitches upward, my butterflies stir.

"There's been all sorts of flags, since I've known you, Lex, that things are weird with your dad."

They're agitated now, twitching all around, and a dampness spreads in my underarms.

"What do you mean?" I ask.

"All those times you stood waiting for him at your swim meets and he didn't show up, the fact that you're fixing this boat for him," he waves his hand behind him, "like it's some kind of competition with your brother to see who'll win the gift-giving contest." He stops, and his gaze burns into me. "It should never be a competition, Lex. Nobody should have to work so hard to be seen, especially by their own father."

His words kick the breath out of me. The old me wants to argue with him, make excuses for why his interpretation is wrong, even though he's exactly right.

"He's the reason you were acting weird when you got the email from Sunridge, isn't he?"

I don't say anything, let his gaze climb all over me.

He nods, like my silence confirms it. "I thought so, because I know what it's like."

The bitter taste of irritation floods my mouth. *How can he possibly know what it's like?*

"What do you mean?" I ask.

"I'm pretty sure my mom is just like your dad."

"But your mom is —"

He shakes his head. "Not dead. I lied about that."

I lurch away from him, unable to hide my shock.

"I tell people she's dead, because nobody believes me when I tell them the truth." His lips press together. "I'm sure you can relate."

He stares at his feet and starts talking, telling me everything he's never told me before.

"My mom and her new boyfriend went away for a week. I needed supplies for a project I was working on as part of my woodworking course. It was late, and I'd left it to the last minute, and the only twenty-four-hour hardware store that had what I needed was a forty-five-minute drive away. I would've taken my mom's car, except hers was at the airport, so I took her boyfriend's car. I knew it was a risk because I only had my learner's permit, but I figured if I took the back roads, I'd be fine. But then a deer jumped in front of my car."

My hand flies to my mouth.

"I woke up in the hospital and the police told me they were charging me with driving without a license — which, fair enough, was true — but also with intent to distribute."

"Intent to what?"

"Distribute. After they freed me from the wreckage, they found a bunch of pills that fell from where they'd been hidden in the wheel well."

My eyes get big.

"Her boyfriend insisted they weren't his. That he had no idea how the drugs got there. That they must be mine."

He pauses, stares at the floor before he continues. "Doing the six months in juvie was nothing compared to realizing that my own mother cared more about herself and her boyfriend than she did about me."

I reach out, let my fingers trail along the raised red line that runs the length of his forearm from his wrist to his elbow, and I know he didn't get it from a mishap with a saw like he said.

"It was the last straw for me — her not defending me. There were lots of other incidents, smaller ones. Ones I could ignore or explain away. But this one made me see who she really was, so after juvie I didn't go back. I reconnected with my dad and Pops, and she was happy to have me gone."

He pins me with his gaze.

"So I get why you did what you did. Why you felt like you had to do what your dad wanted. I get how the need for approval can run so deep that it can change you into someone you don't want to be."

When he says that, something shifts in me, like the change of seasons, subtle but inevitable, but then his voice goes even more quiet, like he's not sure he should say the next part out loud.

"It's taken me a long time to come to terms with the fact that my mother was abusive, and I think you need to consider that about your dad."

The word enters my ear like a snake, searing itself into my brain, and I recoil, like his statement of ridiculousness pushed me. He says it like he knows he's right, even though I know he's never been more wrong about anything.

"I know it's a scary thought," he says. "I didn't want to believe it either, but —"

I race to my father's defense, my loyalty to him surging again, and I loathe myself.

"It's not a scary thought. It's a ridiculous one." I hurl my words at him, hear the edge in my voice. "He's not" — I can't bring myself to use the word he used, the edges of it too sharp to fit in my mouth — "what you said. He's never laid a hand on me."

He looks at me, his eyes heavy with a tired sadness. "Abuse is more than bruises, Lexie."

The lie rolls off his tongue like it's a fact, and I wait for him to realize that he's got it wrong. But he doesn't, and I spend the rest of the night shaking my head, trying to dislodge the snake that won't stop hissing that unspeakable word.

CHAPTER THIRTY

THURSDAY, MAY 16

I show up at Dr. Crowchild's office without making an appointment. Nate's ridiculous word has been wriggling around in my head ever since he said it a couple of weeks ago. I keep trying to unhear it — that awful word he used — but its sharp edges keep poking me like a dried pine needle stuck through my shoe. I need Dr. Crowchild to confirm for me that he's way off base. That while I've never been angrier with Dad, his intentions are mostly well-meaning. That in no way can the *A* word be used to describe how he treats me.

I know she's taking Nate's side, though, when she inhales a breath and then her lips press into a thin line. I feel the word sidle up next to me, dig into me, try to make itself comfortable.

"I have to agree with your friend, Lexie. I didn't use that word when I saw you last, because I didn't think you were ready to hear it. That you were ready to accept that."

"But you can't agree with him because that's not what it is."

I try to explain it again, so she understands better. I listen to myself ramble on and on, explaining why she and Nate are wrong, justifying things the way Dad trained me.

"I get that he's selfish, but most of the things he does, like the business, he does for Jonah and me. So we can do things together."

I say it, but this time when I hear myself say it, it sounds a bit far-fetched, even to me.

She sits up tall and looks me in the eye. "He does it for you? Did you ask to be part of it?"

Her question crashes into me, sends my gut into a spasm. I hold it, rubbing it to calm it down.

"No, but —"

"Did you want to be part of it?"

Her head is tilted to the side and her eyes are squinty. Annoyance brews in me. This wasn't how this was supposed to go. She was supposed to nod and agree with me.

"No," I say, "but him wanting me to be a part of it isn't abusive. Him asking for my help isn't abusive. That's not what abuse is."

I fix her with a stare, daring her to tell me I'm wrong.

"You and Nate don't understand him like I do, and I suck at explaining things properly. I always end up making things sound worse than they are."

She blinks in rapid succession. "But everything you just said is the truth, isn't it?"

I hesitate. This feels like a trick, like the rug's about to be pulled out from under me. I close my mouth, unwilling to admit that what she's saying might be my real truth, because admitting it will make it harder for me to protect myself with the lies I'm so comfortable with.

She levies a pointy stare at me. "If everything you said was true, how could you make it sound worse than it is?"

And there goes the rug. I tumble backward, land with a thud on the very hard surface of reality.

She shifts in her chair, puts her notepad and pen on the table beside her. Her voice takes on a no-nonsense tone.

"You're not wrong in that him asking you for help isn't abuse. Of course it isn't, and each instance of him asking you, or expecting something of you, on its own, can easily be explained away. Each incident is certainly not enough to require a boundary."

She pauses, quietly urging me to hear what she's trying to make me understand.

"But that's how he gets away with it, because it leads to you rationalizing that what he wants from you isn't that bad. That the harmful things he does aren't purposeful, because nobody is perfect —"

"The problem is, Lexie, that you're just like your mother, always blowing every little thing out of proportion."

"— but when you look at it that way, you don't see the whole picture."

She's still talking, but the hissing snake is drowning her out, insisting that I pay attention.

She gets up and retrieves a small cloth bag from her desk drawer.

"Let's say each of his asks is represented by one of these rocks."

She pulls a smooth rock from the bag and holds it up to show me.

"An example might be him asking you to help with one of his jobs after school."

She places the rock in my hand. "How does that feel? Is it heavy?"

I shake my head.

"Of course it isn't. It's one rock. One ask."

She takes it from me and puts it on the table and hands me another.

"That's him asking you to skip swim practice this week. Is that one heavy?"

I shake my head and hand it back to her.

"I think you get the idea," she says. "But what happens when I ask you to hold all of his asks at once?"

She puts the two rocks back in the bag and puts the bag in my palm. She doesn't have to say any more for me to understand the meaning of her demonstration. The snake already told me.

She peers under my eyelashes, capturing my gaze. "Do you feel the weight of them, all at once? Because you're never going to see his abuse for what it is if you look at each incident by itself. It's only when you feel the weight of all of his asks together that you see the enormity of it. It's only then that you see the pattern he's been hiding from you."

Even though her words come out soft and delicate, they're like arrows stabbing my heart.

"Do you see it now, Lexie? Because you can't protect yourself from something you can't see."

I focus on the bag of rocks in my hand and space out my breaths, try to force my voice straight. Happy memories of the dad he used to be flash behind my eyes like a photo album on fast forward. I don't understand how the life I thought I had has come to this. She waits, watching me, endlessly patient.

"But, how can it be" — I search around in my head, looking for any other word — "how can it be called … *that* … when there were so many good times too?"

The tears well up, but I fight them off, force myself to look anywhere but at her.

"It's like if you label it with that word, it erases all the good."

I intend it to be a question, but it comes out like I'm begging, and I hate myself. I try again.

"Don't those times count for something? Because he's never hurt me."

She's quiet for a moment and I feel her kindness envelope me. "Aren't you hurting, Lexie?"

It's when she says that, that a new understanding of my reality creeps into place — one that I know Dad wouldn't want me to know about. A shaking starts somewhere deep inside me, and my tears run down, an unstoppable river of them. A box of tissues appears in front of me and I take one, two, a handful.

"The good times can never excuse the bad, and love and kindness should never be a reward for good behavior. Doing things for others so they'll approve of and love you isn't love."

She pauses, looks like she's trying to arrange what she wants to tell me in a way that won't hurt.

"It doesn't have to be physical to be abuse, Lexie. Abuse is also invalidating someone, dismissing everything that defines them. It's making someone feel tense, so they're always ready to defend themselves. It's ignoring but also blaming someone for everything at the same time, and making them feel guilty for doing things they enjoy. It's ignoring someone's hurt and expecting them to move on like nothing's happened."

She shifts in her seat, but her eyes don't leave mine.

"People who love you should make you feel safe and secure, not tense, and your dad, by refusing to allow you to make your own decisions, criticizing your choices, and blaming you for the things he's done, has destroyed your ability to trust yourself, making you vulnerable and easy to control. He's groomed you to believe that it's your responsibility to support him in every way, regardless of the consequence to you. It's emotional abuse, Lexie. There don't have to be bruises for it to hurt."

As much as I don't want to understand what she just said, I can't help that I do, and I hate that everything she says fits, like the final stroke of color on my canvas, revealing the complete picture of my actual life.

"How do I fix this?" I ask. "How do I make this less hard?"

"You're looking for answers in the wrong place, Lexie. You can't make it better, because it's not about you. None of this is your fault. You're not responsible for your father's abuse of you."

She pauses, lets her words percolate.

"You said you don't trust yourself to make sense of things, and that's normal after what you've gone through. It's going to take time for you to learn how to trust yourself again. The first step is to listen to that little voice inside you, and I don't mean the voice in your head. That voice is connected to what your heart wants to do. It's your gut that you need to listen to, the butterflies, the red flags that beat, warning you of danger. That's your instinct, telling you something isn't right. It takes guts to listen to your gut, but you need to learn to trust it. It doesn't lie."

I swallow her words and file them away, not sure if I'm ready to believe them. I can't help but notice, though, that word is less sharp when I try it out on my tongue, probably because it's no longer hiding under all the lies I believed.

CHAPTER THIRTY-ONE

THURSDAY, MAY 23

I watch nurses, support staff, and visitors come and go from where I try to bury myself in one of the couches in the front lobby. A fresh wave of grief washes over me as I watch a couple of residents play cards, and I wish I hadn't let Mom talk me into coming.

"Lexie." Valerie appears in front of me. "How've you been?"

"Okay. I've been trying not to think about it too much," I say.

"That's understandable. You take as much time as you need before you come back to volunteering, and I do hope you come back."

She pauses to nod hello to some visitors passing through the lobby to reception.

"Mr. Harris left something for you. He insisted that we make sure you have it."

I follow her across the lobby to the nursing station. She reaches over the counter and hands me our Scrabble game and I swallow over a bulge that wrenches up in my throat.

Valerie's hand presses the small of my back. "Sit for a few minutes. I know it's a lot."

She guides me around the counter to the staff sitting area and hands me a bottle of water. Just then, the light indicating that a patient needs assistance lights up. She sighs.

"I'll be right back. We're short-staffed today, so I'm wearing all the hats."

I watch as she disappears down the hall I've gone down countless times before and then lift the lid off the Scrabble box. Of course it's organized as he always organized it. Two bags of tiles — one for vowels and the other for consonants — a sharpened pencil, an eraser, and his little spiral notebook where he kept track of all the words we played and the points we accrued, with our scores tallied on the bottom and circled. I flip through it and can't help but laugh a little when I see the note he wrote after one of our games last year.

Lexie won today, but I didn't tell her. I can't let her think she's a worthy opponent.

I take the long way around the complex to get back to reception, avoiding the hallway that leads to Mr. Harris's old room. The hallway is barricaded though — a maintenance crew had torn open a hole in the wall — so the only way back is to either walk past his room or avoid it by going up the west stairwell and back down the east stairwell to reception.

Get a grip. Just chill out and walk past his room.

Taking a breath to steady the weight of my emotions, I start down the hallway back to reception. I'm just about to walk past his room when the door opens and Zara steps out in front of me. My knees lock and we both stare at each other, neither of us able to find the words that need to be spoken. My thoughts are a scrambled mess of everything that's happened between us, and they play at supersonic speed in my head.

"What are you doing here?" I ask, but as I do I notice that the nameplate beside Mr. Harris's door no longer says "Mr. George Harris," and the devastating answer to her presence in the hallway becomes clear. My eyes meet hers, dark and filled with heartache, and I know I'm not wrong.

"I'm sorry. I should've —"

I can't manage the words and I grab her hand, hoping the gesture says what my mouth can't manage. She squeezes my hand back, her eyes trained on a spot on the floor in front of us.

We're sitting shoulder to shoulder on the edge of Mr. Harris's bed — now her mom's bed. If I hadn't known this was Mr. Harris's room, I'd never have guessed it was his. Zara has hung family photos and cheerful artwork, laid her mom's favorite afghan across the end of the bed, and filled the small shelving unit with books, writing materials, cooking magazines, and a variety of hand creams and lip balms. Folded up against the wall is a walker, and beside it, a wheelchair. The scented wax burner that's always on at Zara's house is here too, cutting through the smell of bleach and smothered air, a reminder of home. It's a remarkable transformation. Mr. Harris never wanted anything on his walls. He said he had the only two pictures he needed on his nightstand.

"You've done an amazing job in here, Zara."

"Thanks. I needed to make this look and feel as much like home as I could."

A tear splashes on her hand, making my guilt rear up, thick and heavy.

"*— wondering if you wanted to help me with it.*"

"This is why you wanted to talk to me, that morning at the pool. You wanted to tell me about your mom, help you get this ready for her, but I was too busy trying to find my phone to listen to you."

"Yeah. But you didn't have the headspace for what I needed to tell you. It was the day after we" — her voice gets squeaky and she stops, collects herself — "the day after we found out that she needed to go into care, so I was a bit of a mess that day."

Her tears come in a rush then, and I fold my arms around her, holding her while her shoulders shake, much like how Nate held me a couple of weeks ago, and try to be who I should've been when she needed me. I remember her baggy, unwashed clothes, her messy bun, her watery eyes. Everything about her screamed that something was wrong, and I hate myself that I didn't give her more of me. That I was so self-absorbed.

"I'm sorry I was distracted," I say.

She turns to face me. "It's my fault too. Since Mom's relapse, I haven't had time to do anything other than take care of her. I missed most of your messages because I was too busy, and I didn't have the mental space to deal with anything else. And I know I could've helped prevent this awful awkward thing between us if I'd just been straight with you, but I felt like I could barely get through a day." She hangs her head. "And then you stopped messaging me altogether. Not that I can blame you, but it hurt that you gave up on me, because I felt like you of all people should have known. Should've asked."

My blanket of guilt spreads itself over me. It's as heavy as lead.

"I know you think it's been about Rhys, but it's not about that. It was at first, but then it just became a good excuse."

"A good excuse?"

She nods. "It was easier for me to have you believe that my problem was about him rather than have to talk about the reality I was facing." She looks me in the eye. "I know that might not make a whole lot of sense."

I nod, not sure how to tell her that it makes perfect sense.

We sit in silence for a long time. Squirrels skitter at each other outside the open window, and squeals of "You're it!" from kids visiting with their parents swallow the silence.

"There are rumors, though," she says, breaking the silence, "about him."

I know what she's talking about. I've heard them too. The most ridiculous one is that the reason Rhys moved here is because he got expelled from his other school after he hacked into their server and changed his and a bunch of other students' grades.

"None of it's true, Zara." I know this because Rhys and I had talked about it when the rumors first started.

"You're sure?"

"I am."

She nods slowly, like she's thinking it over. "I need to ask you something else," she says.

"What?" I ask.

"What happened with Maverick?"

My breath stalls. Her question caught me off guard, even though it shouldn't have. She doesn't look angry about it, but rather curious, and maybe a bit disappointed.

She grabs my hand and squeezes it. "Tell me."

The way she says "tell me" suggests that she knows the answer is going to be a lot. I feel what I've always avoided talking about with her rise in me, along with a slice of fear, because even after everything that's happened, and all the things I know, I also know that I'm not supposed to talk about it, because then the things I'm supposed to believe are at risk of becoming even more fragile.

"I'm not good at talking about it," I say.

"And I was never good at listening, but I'm listening now."

There's a long silence while I search again for the words I can never seem to find. It's like trying to isolate a snowflake from a blizzard. But then I remember how Nate and Dr. Crowchild explained it, and I use the words they used to tell her what I've always tried to tell her but couldn't, and this time she understands me better. Naming the things Dad does makes it harder to find excuses for it. Even the horrible word they used starts to make sense and takes its rightful seat in my vocabulary.

"So I've been a total idiot," she says.

"No. We've both had a lot to deal with."

CHAPTER THIRTY-TWO

WEDNESDAY, MAY 29

Standing in front of the mirror, I work to stuff my hair under my cap and adjust the straps of my new swimsuit. Mom scooped it off a sale rack last week. She's made a habit of scouring the racks for good deals, and this is one of the nicest ones she's found for me. I stand straighter and examine my reflection, pleased that it fits me perfectly, like it was designed for me.

I hope Zara can join me today, especially since the meet's just two weeks away. She said she'd try, but I'm not holding out much hope. I wish I could do more for her and her mom. Mom says that just being her friend is enough. I know she's right, but it doesn't make me feel any less useless.

I close my eyes and focus on what I want to get out of tonight's practice. Despite all the crazy of the last few months, everything I've been working for is finally within my grasp, and I'm not going to let anyone or anything get in my way of claiming it.

The meet is mine. The race is mine. The scholarship is mine. Sunridge is mine.

Coach's back is to me when I knock on his open office door.

"Lexie. Thanks for stopping by. Great swim today. If you swim like that on race day, you'll get that scholarship for sure. No doubt about it."

My heart swells. Not going to lie, I need that money.

"Speaking of that, though" — he grabs a piece of paper from his desk and hands it to me — "your name's not on the list of athletes eligible for a scholarship."

"Why would my name not be on here?"

"They probably just missed it. It's happened before. But I'd take that to their office and ask them to update it with your name. It's important that on the day of the meet, the list is complete."

"I'll run it over there now," I say.

"They close at five. You better hurry."

Granite gray clouds, thick like colored cotton, threaten to unleash their deluge on me as I rush out of the rec center, my hair still wet and smelling of chlorine, and down the road to Sunridge. The admissions office for Sunridge High's School of Fine Art and Music is on the northwest side of the main school, tucked behind a row of tall white maples, their branches tinged with the fresh green of spring. Wind chimes hang from their lower branches, playing their music for the incoming storm. To save time, I duck between the trees and hurry across the manicured lawn to the front door, making it to the admissions office with ten minutes to spare.

A woman with silver hair styled in a bob smiles at me when I walk in. "How can I help you?"

I hand her the list Coach gave me. "My swim coach sent me to ask that this list be updated. My name is missing."

"Sorry about that. What's your name?"

"Lexie Moore."

She sits behind a computer and scrolls through a file. Her eyebrows press together. "Just give me a second."

She takes the list I gave her into one of the private offices lining the wall behind her. She comes back with another woman, about Mom's age, dressed in a cream-colored cheetah print blouse and a black blazer, holding a thick folder. A pair of reading glasses hangs from a chain around her neck. "I understand there's some kind of mix-up here?"

I repeat what I already told the lady with the bob.

She opens her folder, looks at me over the top of her glasses. "You're not eligible for a scholarship without an offer of admission."

My stomach spasms and a wave of nausea rolls through. Suddenly I'm acutely aware of the exact position of every muscle in my body. "But I got an offer of admission. I accepted it."

She flips through the papers in her folder. "Ah. Yes. I see that here. You accepted it on March 12."

A breath of relief escapes my lips.

"But then we received an email from you on March 14 withdrawing your acceptance."

The floor tilts, and my head buzzes like a swarm of bees has been let loose from its hive. My butterflies, their wings inky red, flap furiously, riling up a storm.

"But that's not possible. I didn't send … I wouldn't have sent that."

The confusion on the woman's face deepens. She turns her folder around to show me. "Is this your email?"

It is sent from my email, but I never sent those words. Bile lurches up my throat when I make the connection. Dad had my phone on March 14.

The words coming out of cheetah print lady's mouth are distorted, like they're coming from the depths of a tunnel.

Do you see it now, Lexie? His abuse of you?

"That's not your email?"

A tornado of anxiety turns my guts into slush. "I-it is. But I didn't send that."

She's looking at me, like she thinks I'm lying. "Well then who sent it?"

My Dad did!

I want to scream it at her. The words race up my throat, begging to be heard, but I don't dare let them out, because even though it's the truth, I know I'll sound ridiculous.

People assume that because he's your dad, he'd never do anything to hurt you, but that's how he gets away with it. He wears his Dad camouflage.

She shakes her head in an I'm-sorry-but-there's-nothing-I-can-do-about-it kind of way.

"Since receipt of this email, your place in the program was withdrawn."

I called Dad to ask why he'd done it. Why he'd ruined it for me after all the things I did to help him get what he wanted. After all the things I've done to prove myself to him — to prove that I can be two people, both the me he wants and the me I want. I shouldn't have called, though. I should've known he'd deny it. That he'd somehow make it my fault. Like always. That wasn't the worst part, though. The worst was his I-don't-care tone, the one he uses when he wants me to know that I'm not worth his time. I sat for a while after he hung up on me, mourning the Dad I never had, as if the loss was new, rather than forever, before my grief turned into white-hot fury.

And that's when I ended up here, with freezing water sloshing around my ankles as I shiver with cold. The small crack in the hull that still needs repair, that I made wider by smashing Nate's axe into it, is rapidly gulping up the cold, dark water of the lake.

I flip my hood over my head and stab the water, faster and faster, fueled by the fury churning in my gut, making my blood boil hotter and hotter. I can't hold back the feral scream that erupts from a place deep inside me, and it feels good to let it out. Like I'm somehow freer, lighter.

In the distance, the lights in the marina's shop turn on and a figure steps out. A flashlight sweeps back and forth over the lake before it pins me with its glare. "Lexie! Is that you?" Nate's voice carries clear across the calm water. He sprints to the end of the dock. "What are you doing?"

"I'm taking my dad's boat for a test spin," I yell back.

"Are you insane? It'll sink!"

The water's so cold. Too cold. My legs ache with it. It's licking my knees now, only inches from the boat's rail, my mission just about complete.

"That's exactly the point!" I yell back.

He stands there for a moment, not sure what to do with the crazy I just yelled back at him, before he jumps into action, untying his small fishing boat from the end of the dock. I keep stabbing, faster and faster, fueled by adrenaline and anger and grief, but the more water the boat takes on, the less distance I cover.

"What's wrong with you?" Nate's voice is frantic as he pulls his boat alongside Dad's rapidly disappearing one.

I choke back a sob that surprises me. "You were right, what you said … that word you used. I think he is like your mom." I say the word out loud then, and this time it doesn't get tangled in my throat. "I think he is abusive."

That's all I have to say. Nodding, his mouth a firm line of understanding and resolve, he leans over and grabs my hand. It's strong and warm and safe, and fits my hand perfectly. From the safety of his boat, I reach over and give Dad's boat one last shove, and then watch as the boat I'd hung my hopes on slips beneath the surface, sinking to the bottom where it belongs. I'm not fighting my truth any longer. I'm done trying to be someone I'm not.

CHAPTER THIRTY-THREE

SATURDAY, JUNE 15

Despite the chlorine-tinged humidity that hangs in the air, the air crackles with pent-up energy. It's the kind of energy that makes me swim faster, and I plan to use it to my full advantage today.

Swimmers are gathered in groups along the length of the pool deck, some of them stretching, most of them chatting and bouncing on their heels with nervous excitement. I see the new girl, Charlotte, standing with her team and my insides tangle up with pre-race jitters. I turn away and count and breathe, count and breathe, trying to loosen the tangled lump, determined not to let anything mess with my calm.

It's been seventeen days since I sank Dad's boat and sixteen since I called and left a report with a social worker at our local child protective services (CPS) office. Him sabotaging my spot at Sunridge by pretending to be me was the last straw. After I unloaded on the social worker, she said she was going to call Dad and set up a home visit to talk to him about what I told her. She said she'd want to speak to Mom too. That what I told her was very concerning. I threw up in my mouth when she said that, because it's what I want but don't want. Dad will never forgive me, that I know.

It's also been sixteen days since Mom and Ms. Emerson and I spoke to the Dean of Sunridge admissions about the forfeiture of my application. They wouldn't budge. I tried to explain that it wasn't me that sent the email, but it was as futile as eating soup with a fork. I could see on their faces that they didn't believe me and, worse, that they thought I was a liar. I knew I couldn't blame them because if I were them, I'd think the same thing, but the injustice of it made me press my fingernails into my palms so hard they bled. Now I understand what Nate tried to warn me about.

I focus on the bleachers and my eyes find Mom and Nate at the end, sitting on either side of Zara's mom's wheelchair. It wasn't easy to get her here, but Zara said she refused to miss it. The spot I asked Mom to save for Gran is still empty though, despite the fact that she assured me she'd be here when I called and talked to her two nights ago. I look away, determined not to let her absence interfere with what I'm about to do.

"This is it, girls!" Coach yells from the side. His eyes lock on mine. He doesn't have to say it for me to hear it: *You got this, Lexie. Now go get it.*

I feel the uptick of my heartbeat, the rush of blood in my ears. I suck in a calming breath, grateful for his encouragement, and step up on my block. Zara's standing on the side with the rest of our team, her hands clenched. She mouths "good luck" to me, and I pull my goggles over my eyes, press them into place. Curling the toes of my right foot over the rough edge of the block, I assume my dive position. My heart's punching my ribs now, rapid-fire like a jackhammer, and my muscles tense with the energy that will catapult me forward. It's a stressful moment, but my favorite moment: the split second before the cacophony of sounds erupts and the race begins. The buzzer, coach yelling, people cheering, whistles blowing. I know when it will begin, and when it will end, and what it will look like in between, and I can fight through it, and beat it. It's the kind of chaos that, with practice and training, I've learned to overcome. Although I'll never be able to control it, I have learned to master it.

The buzzer sounds and my body does what it's supposed to, like an elastic band springing forward when its tension is released. When my head breaks the surface I have no idea where I am in relation to the others, but it doesn't matter. I focus on myself, feel my adrenaline surge. My head's down, my elbows are up, and I drive my kick from my hips as hard as I can. As I come to the end of the lane and turn, I know I'm nailing it. I push hard, feel powerful, give it every bit of me I have. I'm closing in on the wall, ten meters to go, and when my hands slam into it and Coach jumps up, thrusting his fist in the air, I know I've done it. I glance at the clock as I choke back a sob of relief, happiness, and gratitude that despite the odds stacked against me I'd still managed to pull it off. I'm a full tenth of a second faster than my personal best. I can't help the happy that beams out of me.

Zara's on her knees at the edge of the pool. She leans over, wrapping me in a bear hug. "You freakin' did it, Lexie!"

"Phenomenal swim, kiddo," says Coach, behind Zara. "You've made a name for yourself after that performance, that's for sure."

I beam up at him, unable to contain the smile that's knocking into my ears, but then my eyes land on Mom, sitting crouched forward with her elbows on her knees, one hand with her phone pressed tight to her ear, the other covering her other ear, trying to block out the noise. My stomach drops. Gran.

"Zara, what's going on? Who's my mom talking to?"

Her face switches. "You need to get changed. Something's happened."

"Are you sure you don't want me to go in with you?"

Somehow I'd gotten myself out of the pool and dressed and into Nate's truck. I heard Nate offer to take me and Mom agreed. I heard Zara promise to represent me and accept my medal if I didn't get back in time. The whole thing feels weird, like I'm watching myself through some other lens. I want to go in and see him because I need to, even though I don't want to. Not after … everything. But what if it's really bad? What if he doesn't make it? Gran said to hurry, that there might not be a lot of time.

The last time I spoke to him was the night I sent his boat to its watery grave. The night I told him that I wasn't interested in the life he was insisting that I live. That I was finished trying to cross oceans to please him, when he won't step over a puddle for me. That I was done trying to make him see me for me. And I meant it. But did I mean it for forever forever?

"I'm sure," I say, forcing an I'm-fine-you-don't-need-to-worry-about-me smile to sit on my lips while my hand flails around for the door handle.

"I'll be here waiting. If you need me."

I want to tell him he doesn't have to wait, but I don't because it's a lie, and I'm getting tired of convincing myself to believe lies I don't believe. Instead, I stumble out of his truck and allow myself to get swallowed up by the swish of the emergency room doors. Inside, I'm greeted with the tired smell of old, pent-up, sick-people air, combined with the acrid smell of too much antiseptic. I take in the waiting room to my right, forcing my eyes over every faded plastic chair, into every corner, but I don't see them. No Gran. No Jonah. No Dad. There's an old man perched in a wheelchair in the corner staring off into space, a woman with limp dull-brown hair wearing bunny slippers and a threadbare pale pink robe flipping through magazines, a child scribbling on a tiny plastic table with the nubs of old crayons.

Maybe this isn't the right hospital?

I approach the information desk, where a receptionist who looks like she's worked a few too many shifts in a row is dealing with a mom who's trying to contain a squirming toddler on her lap. The doors whoosh open behind me again, letting in a blast of warm air, and two paramedics rush past me on the right, pushing a man down the hall on a gurney. My stomach rolls when it occurs to me that the scene likely resembles what played out when Dad got here not too long ago. I'm so focused watching the gurney with the man that could be Dad, I don't notice that the mother with the toddler has left her spot in front of the plexiglass window.

Someone nudges me from behind. "Are you in line?"

"Sorry," I mumble, moving up to sit in the vacated chair. The receptionist waits for me to speak.

I direct my voice through the round hole in the glass, twist my ponytail around my finger. "My dad came in by ambulance. I think he had a heart attack. Is he here?"

"What's his name?"

"Tom Moore."

"Treatment bay 3A, bed 4." She points. I head toward the hall, my eyes on the numbered plaques above the doors.

Hospital workers in scrubs and lab coats hurry past me down the hall. A doctor talks in a hushed voice to a man and woman outside room 2B. The woman's eyes are red and she has a crumpled tissue in her hands, a doll tucked under her arm. I avert my eyes and continue around the corner.

"Lexie." Gran calls to me from a doorway at the end of the hall. "We're in here."

The way she calls my name makes my butterflies take up their flags, stand in a line like an army poised for battle — like what I'm about to walk into might be dangerous.

Dad's sitting up in the bed, fully clothed, looking perfectly normal. Jonah's standing next to him, at the head of the bed, still giggling at something that must have been hilarious. I struggle to make sense of the nonsensical scene in front of me while I try to ignore Gran's gaze, which is raking all over me.

"Your dad's going to be fine. All the tests have come back clear." Dr. Smythe, as indicated by the black name tag pinned to his green scrubs, tells me this, as he steps around me to the space at the head of the bed. I take an involuntary step back as the space seems to get tighter, pushing in on me, and my heart hammers in the hollow at the bottom of my throat.

"What happened?"

"Your dad suffered a bout of indigestion, and compounded with all the stress he says he's been under, it manifested as chest pain."

It's the way Dad's looking at me as the doctor says this, the way his teeth are bared in a tight smile, that makes the full weight of what I've been manipulated to walk into take form in my mind, like a dead bolt sliding into place. I understand, in this moment, that he tricked Gran and me into missing one of my most important moments. His attempts to get me to swallow the blame and apologize for his abuse of me didn't work, and not only did it not work, I dared tell his secrets. I didn't have to be there when the social worker called him and told him what I reported; I knew the rage he felt, and I knew he felt I betrayed him. So he upped the ante and gave himself a fake heart attack. He knew a heart attack would get my attention, play on my heart strings. Get me and Gran to come running. This was all just another lie, another scheme to try to regain control over me. And I fell for it. Hook, line, and sinker.

Slush sloshes in my gut.

Someone who manipulates you and the way you feel doesn't love you. That's called control, and control has nothing to do with love.

Dr. Smythe is still talking. "I'll give you some privacy. The nurse will be by with your discharge papers."

Gran waits for him to leave, then leans over the bed, her voice an icy hiss. "Are you trying to kill your father? First you hurt him by refusing to see him, then you won't help him when he asks, begs you, for help. Did you know he got evicted? Do you even care?" Her knuckles, white, grip the bed rail. "And then, to top it off, you tell a bunch of awful lies. You almost gave him a heart attack!" Disappointment rims her eyes and a piece of my heart dies a little. "Don't you see what you're doing to the family? How could you be so cruel?"

I feel my memory trying to reconstruct itself into something she'll accept, something she'll forgive me for, to fix this, but then I remind myself of what he did, how I know my truth and see without a doubt that it's not me, but him. Taking Sunridge from me, and driving a giant wedge between Jonah and me, and Jonah and Mom, wasn't enough. He took Gran too.

Fighting the hurt that's threatening to spill out of my eyes, I stand taller, gather back some of the power they're trying to take from me.

"I didn't lie. It's not my fault that Dad's version of the truth is different from mine." My voice is clear, my words on point, and the slush that was roiling in my gut has settled. It feels good, empowering.

Gran gasps, her hand flying to her mouth, and Dad's eyes cut me with a glare that, until now, has always been reserved for Mom.

"Forget it," he says, like I'm invisible, a nothing. "There's no use talking to her when she's like this."

"When I'm like what?"

"When you refuse to listen to reason and insist on making me out to be the bad guy. I was hoping we could sort this out like adults and you'd do the right thing and own up to the lies you told, but whatever. What you said means nothing. I've set the record straight with that social worker."

"What do you mean, you set the record straight?"

His lips turn up at the corners and I see the lies that peek out from under them. His eyes are pools of darkness. "I told them all about your mother's abuse of prescription drugs, and how she rages at Jonah. How he's afraid of her, and that's why he's chosen to live with me. Isn't that right, Jonah?"

Jonah nods on cue, and bile bubbles up my throat. I know that nod. I've nodded it a thousand times before. The look in Jonah's eyes belie it though, and it shatters me a little more, knowing that in choosing to put myself first, I've cemented Jonah's inability to do the same.

"They were also concerned to hear that your mother has prevented me from seeing my daughter."

A furious heat rises in me, from my gut to the tips of my fingers, and my body clenches at his audacity, at the lies, at the lengths he's willing to go to punish me. I take a step back, increasing the distance between him and me. "Those are lies. Mom doesn't rage or abuse medications. And you haven't seen me because *I* decided not to see you. I erected boundaries, to protect myself from your abuse."

"Lexie! That's enough!" Gran steps toward me, her rheumatoid-ridden finger pointed at my chest. "You need to leave. Now. Your father's right. You've changed, and not for the better." Tears fill her eyes. "You've already broken your dad's heart, and now you're breaking mine. You're ruining the family, Lexie. Until you apologize to your father for your lies, you're not my granddaughter anymore."

I stare at her a long moment, memories of what was flash like a movie behind my eyes, hoping she'll see through Dad's lies and see me for who I am — for who she's always known me to be — but she doesn't. Dad's replaced her version of me with the version he wants her to see. And then I hear a voice telling me to go, and I realize that it's my gut — my butterflies urging me to see and heed their flags. I hear them and don't look back. And I know for sure that I do mean it: forever forever.

The great puffy clouds that lined the horizon earlier, like boats lined up along a dock, are now streaked with equal parts gray, tangerine, and rose petal pink, the last colors of the day's light. We didn't make it back in time for the awards ceremony at the pool, but in typical post–swim meet tradition, Coach took the whole team for pizza. We always stay as long as we want to, stuffing ourselves with the best wood-fired pizza and virgin cocktails you've ever had.

"You sure you're up for it?" Nate asks when we squeeze into the last available spot in the parking lot. A warm breeze floats in through the open truck window, carrying with it the scent of fresh bread, fire-roasted tomatoes, and Lady Rizzo's famous Parmesan-basil-garlic sauce, and my stomach rumbles. I focus my eyes on a couple of seagulls fighting over a discarded slice of pizza. Another seagull screams at them from above, before it dives down and snatches it from under them.

"I suppose that's a matter of opinion," I say.

A few months ago, my fear of what I walked away from would've destroyed me. I would've done anything to keep the peace, done anything to get him to forgive me and give him reason to keep loving me.

He's shown you who he is. Believe him. That's the truth you need to come to terms with.

But I don't feel that way anymore. Instead, I feel freer now that Gran's shown me the door. Like a weird invisible string that tied me to him is gone. While I'm devastated to lose Gran, I know that if she can't see the truth about who he is and who I am, then, sad to say, it's her loss.

"Well, what's your opinion?"

A tear slips out before I can catch it. It's not a tear of regret, but one of sadness intertwined with relief. "Things are finally going to be all right. For me, anyway."

He moves closer, wraps his arm around my shoulder, and I feel guilty that it feels secure and relaxed, in a way it never has with Rhys, and I don't ever want him to let me go.

"I'm sorry it had to be this way."

I swallow around the lump in my throat. "Me too."

He squeezes my hand, a tiny hand-hug of reassurance, before we head inside the restaurant.

The team's in a private room Coach reserved, sitting around a long table dotted with bowls of garlic bread, salad, and a half dozen different pizzas.

Coach gets up and stands beside me. He looks at me with concern and asks in a low voice, "How's your dad doing?"

"False alarm," I say.

"That's a relief," he says, putting his hand on my shoulder and giving it a reassuring squeeze.

He regards my teammates' faces one by one and says, "Here's our star athlete." He turns back to me. "I hope you're proud of yourself, because I sure am."

"Proud of you? Why would I be proud of you? It'll be your fault if our business falls apart."

"How could you do it, Lexie? You're ruining the family."

"You struggled a few months back, but you pulled it together these last few weeks, and it showed. The scouts noticed you. One from U of A, another from Dal, and one from U of M." His smile is proud. "It's good news, Lexie. Just keep doing what you're doing and you'll get where you want to go. There will be other scholarships in your future."

A surge of emotion smothers my words as I realize that everything I always wished Dad was for me, Coach has been all along. Always encouraging, always supportive, always there. I'd been searching for approval in a place I was never going to find it, and it was right in front of me all along.

It's not about you, Lexie. It's not a reflection of what you're lacking, but of what he's lacking.

"Zara," he calls over the length of the table. "Where's Lexie's medal?"

Zara jumps up from her place at the table, two gold medals swinging around her neck, hers and mine. Her eyes are filled with the thousand questions she can't ask out loud. I return her look with one of my own, and I know she understands. She takes my medal from around her neck and hands it to Coach, who places it over my head, smoothing the ribbon over my shoulders. "You did good, kid. Now let's eat."

Shaking the water from my hands, I push through the bathroom door and crash into Rhys's bandmate Aiden, who's coming out of the men's room.

"I'm so sorry," I say, my still-wet hands pressed into his shirt.

He laughs. "It's okay. Tight squeeze back here. Great swim today."

"Thanks," I say, wiping my hands on my pants.

"How come Rhys wasn't there? Thought for sure he'd be in the front row, cheering you on."

"He couldn't make it. He had his orientation at the Music Academy."

I wasn't happy when he told me that his orientation was the same day as the meet. I couldn't ask him not to go though, since it was me that encouraged him to apply there, as well as Sunridge.

"The orientation is next week," Aiden says. "I'm going there too."

My forehead crunches up. "I was sure he said the orientation was today."

He returns my look of confusion with one of his own. "Maybe I'm the one who screwed up." He flips through his phone, then looks up at me. "Nope. It's definitely next week."

My heart trips.

Wait. What?

Time slows, the noise of the restaurant dulls. I study his face, as if it somehow has the answers to what doesn't make sense.

"Why would he lie?" I ask, but as I ask, it dawns on me, what I didn't know, and my legs go all quivery, like my bones are made of rubber.

"That guy's a walking red flag, Lexie. He's not good for you."

Rhys didn't want to witness my win. Our relationship was all about him. He was just like Dad.

My butterflies kick me, jab me with their flags, making the reality of Rhys, the parts of him I chose to not see so that I could see what I wanted, crystallize in my mind. It's clear to me now what Zara and Nate saw, like a window wiped clean.

The one who claims to love me did not want to see me succeed.

Aiden squeezes past me, like he can't get away from me fast enough, and rushes back into the restaurant.

I slide down the wall until I'm sitting, crouched on the floor, my forehead on my knees, trying to figure out how I allowed myself to care so much about someone who couldn't care any less about me. How I missed the signs that should've been obvious. Out of the corner of my eye, a shadow comes down the hall. It stops in front of me.

"There you are. Can you believe this?" Zara gestures at her lap. "The whole pitcher dumped all over me! It's like cold sticky soup!"

Her mouth keeps moving but I don't hear anything. Everything's echoey.

"Lexie."

She's crouched in front of me now, her face inches from mine. I blink, try to focus on her, but it's like she's wrapped in a fog.

"What's wrong?"

She says more words, but I can't hear anything over the roaring in my head, over the noise of the flapping flags.

She stands up. "You know what? Never mind." She grabs my hand, drags me to my feet. "We're getting out of here."

The three of us are sitting at the end of the dock on an old, unzipped sleeping bag that Nate dug out of the rafters of the shop. Our bare toes graze the still-not-warm lake water. I stare into it, see a frog watching us from its hiding spot between the reeds before it plops back down to hide under the surface of the water. In the distance, thick clouds, their undersides an angry shade of dark, are swallowing up the blue sky, and the breeze carries the humid scent of the coming rain. Zara's more comfortable now that she's changed out of her sticky virgin piña colada–covered pants and is now wearing a pair of Nate's old sweatpants and one of his hoodies. He gave me one too, but I don't feel cold. The truth I can no longer deny is burning itself into every part of me, like it wants to make sure I never forget.

"I don't get it. You both saw how selfish he was. You both warned me about him. Why was I so blind?"

"You can't blame yourself," Zara says. "You didn't see it because you saw what you wanted to see. You ignored what your gut was trying to tell you, what you didn't want to hear, and focused on the good stuff." She pauses, swirling the water with her big toe. "Trust me, I know what it's like. I did it with my mom. I ignored how she got more unsteady, and needed more help getting up and moving around the house." Her voice cracks and I grab her hand. "I made excuses for it because I wanted her — I *needed* her — to get better."

She turns her cheek toward her shoulder and wipes it on Nate's sweater, leaving a wet mark, and guilt washes over me again that I wasn't there for her when she needed me.

"She's right, Lexie," Nate says. "It's hard to see what's hidden in plain sight. You can't blame yourself for being blind to it."

A slow, low thunder rumbles in the distance and a cooler breeze blows through, making the reeds that stand tall along the water's edge sashay against the dock.

"There are some other things about him that you don't know," Zara says. Her eyes scan mine, like she's trying to decide whether or not I can handle what she wants to tell me.

I look away, try to regain control of my heart, which is suddenly jerking around inside my chest. I don't want to know. But I know I need to.

"You can't protect yourself from something you can't see, Lexie."

"It's about those rumors, isn't it? About him cheating?" I ask.

"Yes."

"They're true?"

"Yes. But they're not the worst of it."

I stiffen, will her with my eyes to tell me.

"He's never taken part in a swim meet, never been a top flyer. Probably never tore his rotator cuff. Trust me, I checked and double-checked. My friend Libby did, too. They're all lies."

My blood scrambles, roars through my ears, the truth buzzes around my head, like a saw with no shutoff.

"Wow," Nate mutters beside me. "And he called me a cheater."

Shame snakes through my veins, leaving a trail of slime in its wake, that I ever trusted him, that I didn't let myself see what they saw, at the thought of what I did with him and what I let him do to me, at what I thought I needed to do to prove to him that I liked him as much as he pretended to like me, the way Dad trained me. I wanted to be the girlfriend he wanted. That was most important. It never occurred to me that I should've been more interested in whether or not he was the boyfriend I wanted.

Fat raindrops make divots in the lake's surface, splash against the dock.

I feel Zara's light touch on my knee. "I'm sorry, Lexie."

I duck my chin, unable to respond around the sourness that's burning the back of my throat.

"Are you okay?"

I shake my head, not because I'm not okay, but in frustration that I swallowed so many of his lies without question. Just like I did with Dad's lies.

"Not yet," I say. "But I will be, now that I see."

Dropping my bag at the door, I cross the kitchen to take it from its place in the window. I turn the desiccated stump around in its pot, consider it from all angles. Mr. Harris was right all along when he said that it was hopeless, but I refused to listen to him. Refused to see. The last of its dried leaves have long ago fallen, and lie shriveled in the soil beneath it. I grab it near its base and pull it from the pot; clumps of still-wet soil fall to the floor. It offers no resistance, its roots tiny, pathetic.

Holding it in my hand, I finally understand what Mr. Harris was trying to tell me. It was never about the plant. It was about me recognizing that some things can't be fixed. That despite my best efforts, they'll remain broken, dead, forever out of my reach, just like this hopeless plant.

With the stump tight in my fist, I open the door with my free hand and step outside. A squirrel raiding our bird feeder natters at me in irritation before it hops away to try its luck at the bird feeder two houses over. Then I stretch my arm back behind me like I did so many times with Mav at the park and fling it as hard as I can through the air and watch it sail over the fence, out of my sight, out of my life.

CHAPTER THIRTY-FOUR

WEDNESDAY, JUNE 19

He's already in the pool, just like I planned. I snapped him twenty minutes ago, telling him to just start without me, that I was running late, so that he'd be where I need him to be, so that I can do what I need to do.

I watch him from my hiding spot in the alcove that runs the length of the change room doors. He surfaces at the end of his lane and pushes his wet hair back over his head, in the ultra-confident dickish way that he does. I can't believe I let him help me with my fly, and I wonder again if anything about him is real.

Zara offered to come with me. I almost said yes, but then decided it was better if she didn't. This was something I needed to do by myself. I didn't want to let anyone speak for me, even Zara. I needed him to see me. To hear me.

It's been four days since I swam the swim of my life, was disowned, and then realized that everything about Rhys and me was really just about Rhys, just like everything about Dad and me is really just all about Dad. It took me a few days to find my feet again after coming to terms with how broken Dad made me.

I asked Dr. Crowchild how I could be so blind, given that I should know better. She didn't look surprised, which was a bit annoying.

"Don't be so hard on yourself, Lexie. Your father taught you that red flags and butterflies all look the same, so it's not surprising that you didn't see what your friends saw. It'll take time for you to learn the difference."

It's not something she hasn't told me before, something that I haven't spent a lot of time considering. I realize now that when I was with Dad, I was always on, my butterflies always at attention, prepared to switch gears at a moment's notice, to appease his next whim or mood. Like she said, it's pretty hard to notice that something's a problem when it's part of your regular life.

When he turns at the end of the lane and swims the butterfly back, I step out of the alcove into plain sight. His brow crinkles when he sees me.

"Aren't you coming in?" he asks.

The light, airy butterflies I used to feel when I saw him whip their red flags, scratch the walls of my stomach. I press on them, willing them to settle before I get right to the point. "We're done," I say, pointing back and forth between us.

He hesitates, a beat of annoyance flickers through his eyes. Then he plants his hands on the pool deck and heaves himself out. He stands dripping in front of me. "Is Zara talking crap about me again?"

In my head, I see a dart fly through the air and hit one of those red and white target boards dead center. It was never Zara that was the problem. It was him. It was always him. He twisted it around to make her the enemy.

It's how he gets away with it. He's skilled at making everyone else look like the problem.

My shame for how I let him treat Zara tries to seat itself back on my shoulders, but I shrug it off and stand taller, determined to finish what I came to do and not let him gain the upper hand. "Zara's got nothing to do with this. This is about how you lie and you cheat. About how everything with us is really just about you."

I watch how his gaze shifts, so that he's looking down at me, the way Dad does when he wants to put me back in my place.

"I didn't lie to you. I just made a mistake about the date of the orientation. Why do you have to make such a big deal out of it?"

He smirks, like I'm ridiculous.

A sourness fills my mouth. "This is not just about you not showing up at the meet. We're over."

"Jeez, Lexie. Lighten up. Why do you have to be such a bitch?" He grabs his shirt from the side of the pool and pulls it on.

You were emotionally starved, Lexie. It's not surprising that you latched on to the first person who showed an interest in you.

I see his shirt. It's a red shirt, his *red flag*, reaching to pull me out of the depths of the endless sticky mud, and I feel again, my fingers slip through his.

His lips hook up on one side. "Oh relax. It was a joke."

I take a step back, and then another, needing to get as far away from him as I can before his words can slice into me, leaving me with a scar just like the ones Dad decorated me with. He reaches for me, says something, and I recoil, my back crashing into the change room door. His mouth is still moving when I push my way through it, leaving him and his lies to drip into a cold puddle of his own making.

CHAPTER THIRTY-FIVE

MONDAY, JUNE 24

It's been five days since I called it quits with Rhys, but for some reason he seems to think that our breakup is temporary. I don't see how that's even possible. I think I was pretty clear that we were through, but he's been blowing up my phone for days. I've counted over fifteen apologies, if you can call them that. They're like Dad's apologies. They all come with a "but" attached to them. He's texting again right now, begging me to talk to him, or to at least answer him, to let him convince me about all the excuses he has for lying to me about everything he led me to believe he was. "Please Lexie, I can explain" was one he's sent over and over. That and "Aren't you going to answer me?" Nope. Never. Not even when pigs sprout wings and fly.

CHAPTER THIRTY-SIX

SATURDAY, JUNE 29, CANADA DAY WEEKEND

The usual peat mossy smell of the lake is masked with the competing scents of popcorn, cotton candy, and frying corn dogs as the food trucks get ready for the crowd that's already trickling in. The sky couldn't be bluer or the water calmer. I watch a family of ducks dart in and out of the reeds along the shoreline, next to the dock. A water strider zips around on the surface of the water, making patterns in its wake. It's barely eight thirty and the main parking lot for the beach is already at capacity. Zara, Nate, and I are at the foot of the dock, watching the flurry of people struggle to carry their cardboard boats down the beach to the water's edge, getting ready for the regatta. The small beach has more people on it than I've ever seen. Contestants are tending to their boats, putting last-minute patches of duct tape on areas they missed. Kids are running up and down the wet sand chasing geese, while the younger ones seat themselves in the sand, buckets and shovels in hand.

"Can you believe some of these boats?" Zara says. "Like,

some people took this challenge to a whole other level of crazy. Look at that one."

I follow her gaze to a team of people struggling to carry their boat, which is a not-so-mini version of Noah's ark. It's got windows cut out along the side with animal faces painted next to the cutouts, making it look like the animals are stretching their necks out. Sticking out the top is the head of a giraffe.

"I thought Nate's Gertrude boat and Jonah's motorcycle were a little over the top, but theirs are nothing compared to some of these."

She's not wrong. There's a boat made to look like a float plane, a Loch Ness monster, a giant yellow duck, and another motorcycle. It doesn't have the sidecar though, like Jonah's does. Not that it matters much anymore, since he's not coming, surprise not surprise.

After not seeing or hearing from him since Dad's fake heart attack, he called last night to let me know. To tell me that Dad was taking the day off to help him get his dirt bike running. I wanted to scream when he told me that, scream at the fact that he was still falling for the usual lies, that it wasn't obvious to him that he was being manipulated, that he refuses to see our Real Dad, that he thinks not racing his boat today, the one he slaved over to make it perfect in every way, is something he decided on his own. I wish I could make him see.

Nate moves to stand next to me. He's so close that his arm brushes against mine and a warm feeling runs through me. I don't move away. I like the feeling of him in my space, and it reminds me of a few nights ago when he stood behind me, his chest pressed into my back, when he took my hand in his to show me how to use a spokeshave to shape the transition between the shaft of the paddle he was crafting and its blade. His breath was warm in my ear while he manipulated my hand and talked me through the process, but I didn't hear any of it. I was too busy thinking about the fact that his lips were so close, and that all I had to do was turn my cheek and they'd land on mine. I think it was in that moment that I realized that even though I've always been okay with being just Lexie, his friend, now I think I want to be Lexie, without the just.

"What's wrong?" he asks, interrupting my daydream.

I don't know how he knows to ask, but he always seems to. Rhys never asked. He never knew me the way Nate seems to have always known me.

"Nothing." I pause. "Not nothing. Jonah."

He releases a long, slow breath. "It's not your fault, Lexie. Don't gaslight yourself into thinking it is."

Gaslight. The word Dr. Crowchild used to describe what Rhys did and said to me, after I filled her in.

"When someone tells you it's your fault they behaved a certain way, or blames you for something they did, or tells you that you remember things wrong, or even when they cover up the mean things they say by calling them jokes, those are all examples of gaslighting. It's a form of psychological manipulation used to make you question yourself and your judgment, as a way of gaining power and control over you."

I was stunned, to be honest, and grateful that there was a word to explain all that, because now I have a tangible word I can use to explain Dad's abuse of me.

"You're right," I say, hoping that one day I might believe it. "Thanks for the reminder."

"Welcome, everyone!" A screechy, mechanical voice jolts me out of my head. Roland, the regatta emcee, is at the water's edge, a megaphone pressed to his lips. "All regatta contestants should bring their boats to their designated number indicated on the flags along the water's edge. One of our officials will come around to check that all the boats meet the requirements for taking part. Boats constructed out of anything but cardboard and duct tape will be disqualified."

"I'm impressed that the two of you managed to find this many idiots who wanted to do this," says Zara, stepping farther away from the water, into the shade of a tree.

I shoot a look at Nate. He gives me a slight nod, his way of confirming that yes, we need to tell her. The both of us anchor her with our eyes.

"What?" she asks.

"Jonah's not coming," Nate says.

It takes her a minute, but then it dawns on her. She reacts as expected. "No." She shakes her head back and forth, punctuating every no. "No, no, no, no, nope. I told you. I'm *not* getting into one of your floating death traps."

"Please, Zara," I beg. "We wouldn't ask if we didn't need you, but we need three people: two in Nate's boat and one in Jonah's, and my dad won't let Jonah come."

Her lips pinch together and her nostrils flare. I know it's because of all the things I finally told her about all of it and everything.

"Fine. Tell me what you need me to do."

"Are you sure this isn't going to sink?"

We're sitting in the Gertrude boat, me in front, Zara behind me, ready for the race to start. Nate designed it so that Gertrude will sail as if she's tipped to the side 45 degrees, her front feet in the air on her port side, her ornate wooden trim that runs along her back making the rail on the starboard side.

I steal a glance behind me. Zara's face is a grayish shade of pasty.

"I'm absolutely not sure it won't sink," I say.

"Can't you, for once, just lie and tell me what I want to hear?"

A horn blows. Roland's voice booms through the megaphone. "Boaters! Take your marks!"

"Paddle, Zara, paddle!" I yell over my shoulder.

We were the last boat to set sail because somehow we moored ourselves in the sand after barely leaving the beach, and now Zara's inability to operate a paddle is hindering our progress through the water. It's like every movement she makes with her paddle cancels mine.

"I'm trying!" Her face is scrunched up with the effort of trying to move her paddle as fast as she can, but she looks like a flailing baby bird struggling to make her wings cooperate.

I try to demonstrate, but I'm laughing so hard it's impossible. "You're moving your arms too fast. Try to match my rhythm. Reach farther and pull longer!"

"I'm going as fast as I can!"

A boat that resembles an army tank, complete with caterpillar tracks and a periscope, slides past us on the left, putting us dead last. I glance behind me again and laughter sprays out of me. "Zara! You're making us go backward!"

"It's leaking! My feet are wet! Hurry! We're going to sink!"

She dips her paddle in and out faster, which does nothing for our forward motion, and I let go of my own paddle and bend forward, unable to sit up straight, I'm laughing so hard.

"Lexie! Stop laughing and paddle, dammit!"

Her demands only make me laugh harder.

"I can't breathe." I clutch my stomach. "I can't ... I can't paddle ... like ... this."

"It's not funny, Lexie!" She's full-on shrieking now. "The water's up to my ankles! Paddle! Paddle! Darn it, Lexie, paddle!"

We make it to the other side, barely. By the time we manage to slide into last place, we're sitting in water halfway up our thighs. My stomach aches, and I'll be surprised if Zara still has a voice. Roland walks up and down the narrow beach taking pictures of all the teams, handing out trophies along the way. Zara and I get the trophy for the Most Original Boat That Could Have Won but Sunk, which Nate and I think is the most hilarious thing ever. Jonah's motorcycle comes in second, and again, I regret he's not here. I know he would've been thrilled.

"You see, Zara?" Nate says, his mouth twitching. "I told you we'd see you sail in one of our harebrained death traps."

Her gaze, sharp as nails, cut into him. "Never again," she says, stomping off to find a towel.

"She's never going to forgive us, is she?" he asks me.

"Never. But it was worth it."

Nate cracks up then, and I lose it, all over again.

CHAPTER THIRTY-SEVEN

THURSDAY, JULY 11

"What do I do now?" I ask after I tell Dr. Crowchild everything that's happened since I last saw her. "I feel like I did the right thing, but it's made things so much worse." I bite my bottom lip, the pain a distraction to stop the wave of emotion burgeoning behind my ribs again. "Especially for Jonah."

Dad followed through with his threats and put on his Superman mask to save Jonah from Mom's abuse. The social worker was clueless to the fact that Superman was a fraud, because she called to let Mom know that Dad was going to keep Jonah with him to "keep him safe." It was like everything I confided to her didn't matter. Once again, Dad's lies erased the truth and he got to be the hero.

I fight to force my voice straight. "How can what I've decided to do for myself be good, if so much bad has come from it?"

Dr. Crowchild's face darkens as she listens, but I keep going, determined to finish what I need to say.

"My need to have things be right for me … my, my" — I don't want to say it because I know it's not true, even though sometimes

I still question how not true it is — "my selfishness, failed Jonah and my mom."

Rivers of guilt slide down my cheeks and I dry them on my shoulder. Dr. Crowchild shifts straight in her chair across from me, her mouth a firm, pinched line. I don't need to hear her say what she's thinking, because the me that knows better is saying the same thing.

"It's not your fault, Lexie. You weren't in control of it. You couldn't have stopped it. You're not responsible for it. You're not selfish for wanting to be yourself. I'll keep saying it until you hear me." Her no-nonsense tone is different from what I'm used to, and I know it bothers her, watching me struggle to wear Dad's guilt, like he designed it to fit me. "It's easier to blame yourself, isn't it, than it is to accept that your father, who you love and trusted, betrayed you and your brother."

And there it is. The crux of it. An ache spreads through my chest. I'm pretty sure it's the feeling of my heart breaking as I allow the shield of lies that I wrapped around it, protecting it for so long, to dissolve the rest of the way away.

"Be patient with yourself. You're grieving the father who was always there, yet never was. I know it isn't fair, that it sucks. You deserve to be loved and accepted by your parents, and the freedom to grow into the person you're destined to become. You shouldn't have to prove yourself worthy of love like you've had to, but you don't need his approval to find fulfillment. The only approval you need is the approval you can find within yourself."

She pauses, lets her words settle around me. Almost all of me knows now that she's right. That Dad trained me to not trust myself, to need his approval for everything, so that I'd always be dependent on him. I see now that I can't trust him to do what's best for me, so I need to start trusting myself. I look away from her, focus on the plant in her window, still full of deep purple blooms, while I try to figure out how the truth I've been fighting fits into the shape of the life I want for myself. A box of tissues appears in front of me. I take one and blow my nose, buy a few seconds to arrange my thoughts.

"There's just one thing that keeps bugging me," I say.

"And what's that?"

It takes me a while to get the words out, because they're illogical. Ridiculous, even.

"I miss him," I say, my voice a whisper. "Isn't that crazy?" My voice gets louder, turns shrill. "What does that say about me? He sabotaged and disowned me, turned my grandmother against me, and stole my brother." My eyes fill with angry tears again, and wipe them away, hating them and what they represent.

Her eyes are rimmed with empathy. It's the same look Mom wears when her concern for me is paired with defeat. "You're only craving what you're entitled to. It's a hard thing to rationalize, when it's the ones we love and trust that hurt us, but you need to understand that just because someone hurts you doesn't mean that you stop loving them. One doesn't preclude the other. It's not crazy at all."

What she says makes sense, even though it doesn't. Not really. "I just wish ... I wish —"

"What do you wish?"

"I wish he could be who I need him to be," I say.

"Of course you do. And that's going to be the hardest thing for you to accept. That he never was who you thought he was."

The memories of what I thought he was roll down my cheeks. I wipe them away to nothingness, much like the hopes they carried in them.

"Do you think I did the right thing, walking away?"

"It's not a question of whether or not it's the right thing, but rather, if you feel that you're entitled to be yourself or not. Whether or not you feel you can put your own happiness ahead of his priorities. Nothing you do will make him be the person you want him to be, and you don't have to be anyone you don't want to be."

I stare into my lap, feel the weight of her words. Let them become real in my head.

"The steps you've taken are necessary for you to choose yourself, for you to be your authentic self, and not the self your dad chose for you. Do you understand that?"

I nod. I think I do understand what she and Nate have been trying to tell me. What they've forced me to open my eyes to.

"And if you're going to move forward and recover from this, you also need to understand that it's impossible to heal from an abusive relationship when you're still trapped in an abusive relationship." Her gaze catches mine and holds tight. "So yes, it's okay and in fact necessary to walk away from a toxic family member. You're worthy of love and having a life of your own."

The house is quiet. Mom's at work. I've done the dishes, put the laundry away, and taken out the garbage. Now I'm sitting at the kitchen table with my sketchbook, a mallard's feather, and a selection of my graphite pencils, letting what Dr. Crowchild said percolate. Using my HB pencil, I work to sketch out the barbs of the feather, drawing lines from the rachis outward. Then I use my 4B pencil to create darker tones, increasing the contrast. I work my way down the drawing from top to bottom, noting that the barbs at the top are darker and more rigid than the ones at the bottom, which are softer and lighter in color. I work up and down, alternating my use of my pencils and the pressure I place on them, trying to get the value and directional stroke just right. It's my attention to these details that quiets the noise in my head, letting me sort the good from the bad, the facts from the fiction, the unquestionable from the questionable, and a quiet acceptance seeps in, gets comfortable in my consciousness, like it knows it belongs there.

"Nothing you do will make him be the person you want him to be, and you don't have to be anyone you don't want to be."

She's right. I've been fighting it for a long time, but I see now that my relationship with Dad isn't normal, that it is abuse, and I don't have to accept it. There isn't something wrong with me or us, but something wrong with him. I have my boundaries and I see the flags. Now all I have to do is let myself be the me I want to be.

CHAPTER THIRTY-EIGHT

WEDNESDAY, JULY 24

I climb up on the diving block and shake out my arms and legs. Now that I've shaved a tenth of a second off my time, I'm working on the next tenth. I stare at my reflection in the water and see what I always see: strong, muscled shoulders, sleek, long legs. But this time I also see a different me. This time the me that stares back looks confident. Determined. Satisfied. Like she knows what she wants, and isn't afraid to go get it. Like the girl she was destined to be.

Eleven days ago, I got the call that I've been hoping for. I'm pretty sure I deafened the poor woman who called with my scream of yes, and then when I told Zara, she deafened me. I've saved every penny I've earned for the tuition I've been hoping to pay for, working my regular shifts at the marina, and then helping at the OldMill in the evenings, so I think I should have almost enough to cover at least the first semester's tuition. I feel lighter now, like a weight I've been carrying around forever is somehow gone, and I know it's because finally things are going right for me. Everything I've worked for is working out.

I sent Dad a text, telling him that I was reoffered my spot and that I accepted it, and that I hoped he'd be happy for me. Mom insisted I tell him. That it would look bad on her if I didn't, especially now that child protective services is watching.

I'm not surprised that he didn't respond. I try to convince myself that his silence is better than his harassing texts and gaslighting, but I can't help feeling abandoned all over again, and I try not to let the immense noise of his silence erase the burgeoning smidgen of approval I've allowed myself.

"Do you see it now, Lexie? Because you can't protect yourself from something you can't see."

I'm about to dive in, shatter the perfect mirror beneath me, when my phone chimes his chime, and the relaxed confidence I was enjoying rushes out of me, like water rushing from a broken dam. Red flags scrape my intestines, making them knot together. Stepping off the block, I grab my phone from my bag and click on his message.

I'll be here waiting for you when you wake up and realize that your mother put silly ideas in your head, forcing you to want something you don't need, as a way of interfering in our relationship. I don't blame you for being mean and pushing your brother and me away. I love you.

A flaming red rage rips through me, scorching hot, making me vibrate with a ferocity unlike anything I've felt before. I grip my phone tight, press it under my arm so I can't whip it at the wall and watch his latest attempt to gaslight me smash into a million bits. Leaning forward, my hands on my knees, I count and breathe, count and breathe, forcing calm, restraint. It takes an Everest-sized mountain of self-control to not text him back with a response of my own: to call out his lies; to point out that his accusations are a reflection of his own crimes against Jonah, Mom, and me; to let him know that I have a solid grasp on my truth and I will no longer allow him to gaslight me; to tell him that I see him for who he is, and I can't unsee it. I don't do it though because that's what he expects me to do, what he *wants* me to do. It's my anger that allows him to slither between my boundaries, allows him to keep laying the blame of our non-relationship at my feet. I see the pattern now, the game he wants me to play. Instead, I slam myself into the water and I swim, hard and fast. I pound the water with my fists, lap after lap, one, three, ten, a thousand. I don't care about my form, I just need to pound the crap out of something and the water, I know, will forgive me.

CHAPTER THIRTY-NINE

TUESDAY, AUGUST 6

It's just before seven a.m. My intention was to get here early, before it gets too hot, but it's the kind of weather that holds the heat, where the air is so thick it feels like you could cut a wedge of it out with a knife and serve it with a side of whipped cream. The dampness clings to every surface. Even the cattails that usually stand straight and tall, protecting the marsh, look weighed down, their heads heavy, slanted sideways, like they're reaching toward the cool water for some relief. My hair does the opposite, though. I can feel it curling, lifting from my scalp, encasing my head in a wide, frizzy helmet. Gathering it in my hands, I twist it around on itself and secure it into a messy bun on top of my head, and focus on the swans, the reason I'm here. They're the subject of my eighth sketch, my second this week, in the sketchbook I started four months ago. It's my third morning in a row sitting on the grassy bank, trying to capture mama swan's gracefulness, along with the playfulness of her cygnets as they zigzag in little lines behind her, doing their best to keep up. I've promised myself that I'm going to fill up this sketchbook, continue to build my portfolio, keep working to improve my craft. I also promised myself to not tear out any pages. I used to do that when I wasn't happy with my work, but I've realized that Ms. Wilcox is right. I should keep them all, crappy or not, because it's a record of my improvement, and all good sketchbooks have bad sketches.

"You look like you could use some water," Nate says from behind me, making me startle. He holds a glass out to me, dripping with condensation. "Sorry. I didn't mean to scare you."

I take it and gulp at it greedily, the ice clinking against my teeth. "It's okay. I was so focused on trying to get her plumage right, I didn't hear you behind me."

He crouches beside me, leans into my space to study my work. Despite the heat, goosebumps race up my arms. I study his profile, notice the fine stubble along the curve of his jaw, and the way the fringe of his hair brushes the top of his long eyelashes. He's so close, close enough to kiss me, and I wonder what it would be like. He's not ultra sexy, in a Rhys way, but he is, in a rougher, more rugged way. A better way. He lets himself sink back, catching himself with his hands, to fall in next to me, and my stomach gets a loose feeling, like it might float away. I close my pencil in my sketchbook and tuck it behind me.

"I picked up the marina's mail yesterday," he says, pulling an envelope from his back pocket.

I make a face. "More bills?"

He hands me the envelope. "Not this time."

Concerned, I take it from him, but my heart quickens when I see the return address. It's from the publishing department of *The New York Times*. Tearing the letter from the envelope, my eyes race over the page.

"He did it! He's going to have his puzzles published in *The New York Times*!" I laugh-yell, making mama swan dart farther into the safety of the marsh. I press the letter into my lap, unable to contain the grin that's taken over my face. Nate's eyes lock on mine. They're soft, shining.

"It was you, wasn't it? I knew it had to be you," he says, answering his own question. "I told you to just leave them, that I'd deal with them later, but you didn't listen to me."

I shrug an it-doesn't-matter shrug. "You were so busy and worried. I figured there was no harm in trying. The worst that could happen is that they'd say no, but the best that could happen is … well … this!" I allow my eyes to scan the letter again. I need to make sure it's real, real.

"This would have meant so much to him. I'm glad you didn't listen to me." His voice is higher than normal, but I pretend not to notice. "And you doing this, seeing this dream of his through for him, proves to me even more that you are" — his voice trails off — "exactly who I've always known you to be."

His gaze grabs hold of mine again, tugging me in, and tiny sparks race up and down my spine.

"So it's only fair that you be the one to use the payment from the publisher, to help you pay for your tuition."

He hands me a check and I gape at him. It's worth twenty-five hundred dollars.

"I can't accept —"

"It's a loan, Lexie, and yes you can. You need it more than us right now. And it's the least we can do, given all you and Zara did to help me and my dad and Pops get this place" — he holds his hand up and casts it in an arc in front of us — "to where it is now. We couldn't have pulled this off without you." He pauses, hooks my ankle with his foot. "And, if it wasn't for you, and your courage to tell me what your dad did to us …"

I try not to cringe at his choice of words, but I get now that he isn't wrong. The old me would've been too scared to say anything about Dad. The consequence would've been too great. But with his help, I've come to see that the long-term consequence of the alternative would've been far greater.

"We would've lost everything." His eyes plead with me. "Let me help you get where you want to go, Lexie, like you helped us."

Everything about him, and the vulnerability of the moment, makes something in me come undone, and I sink into him, letting his arms wrap around me, where they fit, exactly how they should, like the way a wave fits in the ocean, and I can't help hoping that the moment never ends, and that he doesn't want it to either. I lift my chin to meet his gaze, his face inches from mine. "Okay," I say.

And then his lips do find mine, and my heart feels lighter than air, like it might float away and follow the curve of the endless sky, and I know deep in my bones that what I feel right now is 100 percent more right than anything I ever felt with Rhys.

CHAPTER FORTY

TUESDAY, AUGUST 20

"Table for how many?"

A group of four adults and two small kids stand in front of me. The little girl of about five clutches tight to the doll she has tucked under her arm, while her toddler-sized brother tries to wrestle it away from her. Their mom bends at the waist to whisper in his ear, which stops him, but only momentarily before he starts again, this time successfully yanking the doll away from his sister, who yells out in alarm. One of the other adults in the group steps closer, away from the commotion, and asks for a table for six, and could they please sit outside, under the pavilion on the dock. I count four menus and grab enough paper and crayons for two kids, and have the group follow me, the doll back in its rightful place under the little girl's arm, the boy tucked tight under his mother's, his screams of indignation carrying over the lake.

Imani called in sick today, so I'm covering the breakfast rush at the OldMill instead of working my usual shift at the marina. It's been a hectic summer, but thankfully Nate's dad was able to hire more people. Since the regatta and the grand opening of the OldMill, the marina almost never has canoes sitting empty, and there hasn't been a night that the OldMill hasn't been packed. The next step in realizing Pops's dream is renovating the motel portion of the OldMill, but like Nate said, there's no rush on that.

I'm passing menus around the table when Nate leans into my ear. He smells good, like a mix of sandalwood, sage, and citrus rolled into one. My stomach hitches, as I revel in the memory of how his lips feel on mine. I'm still amazed at how easy it is with him. There's no work involved, like there was with Rhys. It's like we fit together, like dandelions and daydreams, and it makes the fakeness of Rhys even more indisputable.

"There's someone at the front asking for you."

"Who?"

The little boy's mom is trying to stuff his wriggling legs into a high chair, but he arches his back and lets out a wail.

"No idea. Just asked if you were here."

I turn back to the family and tell them that their server will be with them momentarily before heading back to the front. A blond woman wearing a navy pantsuit, a zipped black leather case held to her chest, is standing there. I study her and her crisp no-nonsense outfit, not able to hide the curiosity that I know is written all over my face.

"I'm Lexie," I say. "Can I help you?"

She hands me her business card. "Lindsey Abbott. I'm a lawyer with Abbott and James. Can we talk?"

I'm sitting on my trembling hands across from her, in a booth tucked away from the crazy of the main dining room, my red flags rigid, ready. A million thoughts swim through my head, making tremors quake up and down my spine.

Is this about the lies he told the CPS worker? Is she here to tell me that I can't go to Sunridge, that I have to live with him, that I have no choice but to do what he wants?

Do they know it was me that made his fake license and insurance papers? Did he tell them, like he threatened he would if I told anyone? Will that give me a criminal record? Is that why I need a lawyer?

I count in my head, anything to distract myself and avoid upchucking on the table in front of this woman.

"You must be wondering what this is about," she says, unzipping her case.

I nod. It's all I can manage.

She pulls a file from her case and slides it across the table toward me. "I'm the executor of Mr. George Harris's will."

I blink, my heart snags. *What?*

"I understand you knew him well?"

My chin lowers to my chest, a barely there nod.

"He's left some of his estate to you, to assist you in paying for your postsecondary education, and" — she reaches across the table and points at a line near the bottom of the second page — "for any tuition required should she be accepted into Sunridge High's School of Fine Art and Music."

My chest seizes, air knots in my throat.

Estate? Tuition? What?

She turns the page and points at something else, but I don't see it through the fog of tears clouding my vision. She says more stuff, I know, because she's turning pages and pointing, but I don't hear or see any of it. All I can think of is Mr. Harris, and what he's done for me, and I understand in a way I didn't before that despite his gruffness and sharp-edged criticisms, he was rooting for me to take charge of me, that he believed in me in a way that my own father never has. I blink a tear free and can't help noticing the irony: Even though he's gone, he's still looking out for me, while my father, who's alive and well, can't be bothered to know me. It makes my heart happy and sad at the same time.

"So that's it," she says. "I'll be in touch with you in the coming days regarding the logistics of the transfer of the funds." She pauses, looks at me. "He told me about a brilliant girl who played Scrabble with him. I've been his lawyer since his divorce over twenty years ago. You should know that he loved you. You filled a big void for him. I'm not sure if you knew that."

She gathers the file and zips it back into her folder.

"His only daughter never forgave him when he later married his partner. Him coming out and living as he wanted to, with the man he loved, cost him his relationship with her and her daughter, his granddaughter. I have no doubt that he saw you as the granddaughter he wasn't allowed to have, and that's why he's left this for you."

She stands to leave. "Do you have any questions for me?"

I shake my head, my words tangled up inside the lump of grief and gratitude that clogs my throat.

I stay sitting where she left me, too stunned to move, like I'm shackled by the weight of all the feelings, when she's at my side again, a plant full of bright red blooms in her hands.

"I almost forgot to give you this," she says, placing it on the table in front of me. "He was very insistent that I gift you a new plant. And it had to be one bursting with bright new flowers."

A sob chokes its way up my throat and I cover my mouth.

She rests her hand on my shoulder. "He also insisted that I include that card with the plant." She points between the healthy, plump, bright green leaves.

I slide the card out of the tiny envelope, his last message to me forever captured in his familiar blocky handwriting:

Water this one. It's not dead.

I laugh and cry at the same time.

CHAPTER FORTY-ONE

SEPTEMBER

The artist's garden is woven with a cobblestone walkway that creates a meandering path to the front doors of the School of Fine Art and Music. Giant hydrangeas lean over, unable to hold high their giant blooms of pink, white, and lavender — now even heavier with the morning dew — from filling the spaces lining the path. The walkway is punctuated by various works of art: a statue of a bear climbing a tree, an inukshuk, deer and fox sculptures made of sheet steel, and a set of wind chimes made of sea glass that tinkles in the slight breeze of the morning, carrying with it the sweet rose and citrusy scents of the flowers. The middle of the garden hosts a navigational sign atop a bright red post that reads, "This way to inspiration," and a banner stretches over the main walkway, welcoming new students. I blow out a breath. I made it. I did it. I'm here.

The two of us — or rather the three of us if you include Mav — are sitting in a puddle of shade offered by a maple tree, Mav using his paw to try to trap a grasshopper that's trying to escape. Zara didn't tell me that Mav's awesome new family returned him to the rescue. Apparently he wasn't very good at getting along with the chickens on their farm; seems he saw them more as prey than his farm friends. So it was a shock when I walked into the marina three weeks ago and he ran at me, crashing into my knees in the way he always did. Nate and his dad decided to adopt him. They could now, given that their finances were better.

Nate rests his hand on my knee, the weight of it offering a comfort I didn't know I needed. "You good?"

I feel the all-too-familiar lump rise in my throat. Being here, and having Mav back, softens the grief that still lingers, like a sticky cobweb stuck in the nooks and crannies of my mind, close enough to remind me of its presence, but too sticky for me to sweep it away entirely.

"Of course. This is what I wanted." I look away from him, not wanting him to see the regret that still hides under the surface of my success. It's taken me a long time to accept that Dad is who he is, and to be okay with the fact that I don't need him in my life to be fulfilled, and that in many ways, I'm better off without him.

I just wish that the same was true for Jonah. He's still caught up in Dad's lies.

Mav shoves his nose under Nate's arm, wedging himself between us. I scratch his neck and he flops over on his back, tongue hanging out.

"You should go," Nate says. "Don't want to be late on your first day."

He shifts back, leans into me, like he wants to tell me a secret. His breath is warm on my cheek and he smells good, like fresh rain, and my butterflies float up. They're the good kind, though. I can tell the difference now. These are the delicate, airy ones that dance lightly and tickle my insides, making me feel warm and cozy. Mav rolls out of the way then, as if on cue, distracted by a moth, and I turn my head slightly, letting his lips find mine. My lips part as I kiss him back, and he tastes like cinnamon and mint, and it feels like it should: safe and warm and right, and I don't ever want it to end. I'm grateful that I was able to recognize what was in front of me all along. This love isn't hot and heavy or pushy or demanding. I don't feel like I have to do things to make him happy, to be someone I'm not to get him to stay. He doesn't tear me down, make me do things he himself is afraid to do. He listens, is always interested, always there for me. He sees me for me. Loves me for me.

A bell dings from somewhere inside and he pulls away. "That's your cue."

I stand up, throw my backpack over my shoulder, and lean down to scratch Mav behind his ears. I'm rewarded with a slobbery wet kiss before I head into the school and the life I chose for me. It's taken me a long time, but now I get it, in a way I never did before. There's no room in my relationship with Dad for the both of us. It's either him or me, and I choose me. It's not the choice I wanted to make, but the one I had to make, and even though everything's not okay, I know everything will be okay, for me, because now I'm free to be the me I want to be, and boy, does it ever feel good.

A PROMISE FROM ONE WRITER TO ANOTHER

BY MARSHA FORCHUK SKRYPUCH

Sheryl and I became friends after meeting in 2017 at a SCBWI lunch gathering for children's writers, both published and aspiring. She joined Kidcrit, my online critique group, and since we both lived in Brantford, Ontario, and both enjoyed walking, we'd get together a few times a year for long walks and to pick each other's brain about what we were writing. We also went out to dinner with our husbands in tow.

In the fall of 2022, Sheryl told me her terrible news, that she had recently been diagnosed with terminal cancer and was having her first chemo the next day. She wanted to spend every possible minute that she had left with her three sons and her husband. But she had just finished what she called a "messy first draft" of *Red Flags and Butterflies* and wondered if I knew someone who could "finish it" for her … "you've always given me great advice that I've taken to heart," she wrote. "Hoping you have just one more great idea."

In this horribly devastating time for Sheryl and her family, there was one promise that I could give her: that I would either find someone to finish her novel or I would do it myself. I also offered to sit through chemo with her if she wanted, or to do errands, or be a listening ear. She just had to ask.

When I read the state of her current draft, I was wowed. This was no messy first draft. It still needed work, but it was almost ready to submit to publishers. I told her I could do the polish, but that it was so close to finished that she might want to do it herself.

We met in coffee shops to untangle story knots and talk about tweaks. I didn't want to overwhelm and was ready to step in if necessary, but working on her manuscript became a respite from her grim diagnosis. We continued to meet and talk story-smoothing, and by November 2023, her novel was ready to be seen.

I emailed Barry Jowett, who was the editor of my first three novels. I told him about *Red Flags and Butterflies*, but was upfront about Sheryl's circumstances. It can be difficult for a publisher if an author dies before a book has completed the publishing process: there are several more edits to go through once a story has been accepted, there's promotional material to prepare, and so on. But Barry and I had worked together through three novels, plus I knew this novel well. I assured Barry that I would and could step in if necessary. He agreed to clear his plate and read the manuscript quickly.

Sheryl submitted it and Barry loved it, which I knew he would. He sent her a contract at the end of January 2024. Despite failing health, Sheryl was able to complete her promotional material. Sheryl held her book contract in her hands. She was thrilled. She told me that if her book helps even just one reader, she will have achieved her goal.

She died in March 2024.

Sheryl's final edits were done by me.

ABOUT THE STORY

It is a testament to Sheryl's compassion and talent that she could write such an authentic novel about domestic abuse when she had not been a victim of it herself. *Red Flags and Butterflies* was inspired by true accounts. Sheryl was a staunch advocate for Keira's Law, Bill C-233, named in memory of one young victim. The law requires federal judges to be educated on intimate partner and family violence.

Sheryl's goal with this book was to empower young people, help them understand their own worth, trust their instincts, and change their internal dialogue to create a healthier, more positive mindset, particularly when it is a loved one who causes them to question these things about themselves.

RED FLAGS

In *Red Flags and Butterflies*, Lexie is subjected to emotional abuse by her father and her boyfriend. She extricates herself once she recognises the red flags that mean danger.

What are some of the red flags of emotionally abusive behavior in this story?

Lexie's father piles her up with chores that benefit him but will stop her from achieving her own goals in life. His **selfishness** is a red flag.

Rhys lies about being kicked out of his previous school and pretends to be a competitive swimmer. His **lies and inflated self-image** are red flags.

Her father adopts a puppy and guilts Lexie into spending more time at his place because otherwise the dog will be neglected. **Using guilt to manipulate** is a red flag.

When Lexie finally confronts Rhys over his lies and selfishness, he cannot apologize. A person who **can't say they're sorry** is a walking red flag.

Lexie's father tries to reframe their shared past in a way that makes him the victim. This is **gaslighting** and a big red flag.

If you have red flags in a relationship, you can get help. Talk to your school counselor or a trusted adult. In Canada, you can call the Kids' Help Phone at 1-800-668-6868 for 24/7 free and confidential care for Canadians aged 5 to 29, or visit kidshelpphone.ca.

ACKNOWLEDGEMENTS

With great pride and deep emotion, our family is honored to see Sheryl's book being released. Though Sheryl is no longer with us, we know she would be filled with hope that her words might make a difference in a young person's life. When Sheryl was diagnosed with cancer and told she was immediately palliative, she feared she might not have the time or strength to finish her manuscript. Thankfully, the treatment offered her more time than expected — not just to continue writing, but to find moments of focus and purpose amid the challenges she faced. The book became a welcome distraction and a source of comfort, allowing her to channel her energy into a story she believed in deeply. She worked hard to shape and refine it, and was ultimately able to place it in the hands of those who could help bring her dream to life.

This book would not have come to life without the support and encouragement of many. We would like to express our gratitude to Marsha Skrypuch who was especially instrumental — not only in encouraging Sheryl to begin writing this story years ago, but also for her mentorship through the early stages via KidCrit. Marsha, your support meant the world to Sheryl, and we are endlessly thankful to you. Thank you, Brian Henry of Quick Brown Fox whose feedback was extremely helpful. We are also deeply grateful to Barry Jowett, who recognized Sheryl's talent, and to the teams at Cormorant Books, DCB Young Readers, and copy editor extraordinaire, Fei Dong.

Jennifer Kagan-Viater — whom Sheryl came to know through her advocacy for women and children — and her daughter, Keira, whose life was heartbreakingly cut short, powerfully underscored the urgent need for a story that sheds light on coercive control within families. Though extreme, their experience, along with the many anonymous stories Sheryl encountered through support groups and resources dedicated to supporting victims and survivors, fueled her determination to complete this novel. The relationships made were deeply meaningful to Sheryl.

Finally, we want to thank Sheryl herself — our beloved wife, mom, daughter, sister, aunt, and friend. Though she is no longer with us, her love, warmth, and generosity continue to echo through every page of this book. She gave so much of herself to those around her, always listening, always caring, and always valuing the thoughts and feedback we shared with her as she brought this story to life. We will forever cherish the time we had with her — our walks, our visits, our long chats — and we carry her spirit with us in everything we do. This book is a reflection of her heart, and we are honored to share it with the world.

PHOTO CREDIT: JOSEPH AZZAM

Sheryl Azzam lived and raised her family in Brantford, ON. A medical and scientific writer by profession, she completed her novel shortly before her passing, aiming to help young readers recognize moments when those meant to love them don't have their best interests at heart. Above all, she cherished her family — her husband, three sons, and their two beloved dogs. Her legacy of love, strength, and compassion continues to inspire all who knew her.

We acknowledge the sacred land on which Cormorant Books operates. It has been a site of human activity for 15,000 years. This land is the territory of the Huron-Wendat and Petun First Nations, the Seneca, and most recently, the Mississaugas of the Credit River. The territory was the subject of the Dish With One Spoon Wampum Belt Covenant, an agreement between the Iroquois Confederacy and Confederacy of the Ojibway and allied nations to peaceably share and steward the resources around the Great Lakes. Today, the meeting place of Toronto is still home to many Indigenous people from across Turtle Island. We are grateful to have the opportunity to work in the community, on this territory.

We are also mindful of broken covenants and the need to strive to make right with all our relations.